# AT HOME WITH
# THE JARDINES

## LILIAN BELL

1st WORLD
LIBRARY
Literary Society

# At Home with the Jardines

## Lilian Bell

© 1st World Library, 2007
PO Box 2211
Fairfield, IA 52556
www.1stworldlibrary.com
First Edition

LCCN: 2007927840

Softcover ISBN: 978-1-4218-4555-5
Hardcover ISBN: 978-1-4218-4471-8
eBook ISBN: 978-1-4218-4639-2

Purchase *"At Home with the Jardines"*
as a traditional bound book at:
www.1stWorldLibrary.com/purchase.asp?ISBN=978-1-4218-4555-5

1st World Library is a literary, educational organization
dedicated to:

- Creating a free internet library of downloadable ebooks

- Hosting writing competitions and offering book publishing
scholarships.

Interested in more 1st World Library books? contact:
literacy@1stworldlibrary.com
Check us out at: www.1stworldlibrary.com

# 1ˢᵗ World Library Literary Society

## Giving Back to the World

"If you want to work on the core problem, it's early school literacy."

**- James Barksdale, former CEO of Netscape**

"No skill is more crucial to the future of a child, or to a democratic and prosperous society, than literacy."

**- Los Angeles Times**

"Literacy... means far more than learning how to read and write... The aim is to transmit... knowledge and promote social participation."

**- UNESCO**

"Literacy is not a luxury, it is a right and a responsibility. If our world is to meet the challenges of the twenty-first century we must harness the energy and creativity of all our citizens."

**- President Bill Clinton**

"Parents should be encouraged to read to their children, and teachers should be equipped with all available techniques for teaching literacy, so the varying needs and capacities of individual kids can be taken into account."

**- Hugh Mackay**

TO

Dr. John Sedgwick Billings, Jr.

AND

Dr. John Clarendon Todd

WHOSE COURAGE, SKILL, AND WISDOM

SAVED A PRECIOUS LIFE

# CONTENTS

# CHAPTER I

## MARY

I have never dared even inquire why our best man began calling my husband the Angel. He was with us a great deal during the first months of our marriage, and he is very observing, so I decided to let sleeping dogs lie. I, too, am observing.

It is only fair to state, in justice to the best man, that I am a woman of emotional mountain peaks and dark, deep valleys, while the Angel is one vast and sunny plateau. With him rain comes in soothing showers, while rain in my disposition means a soaking, drenching torrent which sweeps away cattle and cottages and leaves roaring rivers in its wake. But it took Mary to discover that the smiling plateau was bedded on solid rock, and had its root in infinity.

Mary is my cook!

Yet Mary is more than cook. She is my housekeeper, mother, trained nurse, corporation counsel, keeper of the privy purse, chancellor of the exchequer, fighter of exorbitant bills, seamstress, linen woman, doctor of small ills, the acme of perpetual good nature, and my best friend.

Cheiro, when he read my palm, said he never before had seen a hand which had less of a line of luck than mine. He said that I was obliged to put forth tremendous effort for whatever I achieved. But that was before Mary selected me for a mistress, for Mary was my first bit of pure luck. Our meeting came about in this way.

We were at the Waldorf for our honeymoon, which shows how inexperienced we were, when a chance acquaintance of the Angel's said to him one night in the billiard-room:

"Jardine, I hear that you are going to housekeeping!"

"Yes," said Aubrey, "we are."

"Has your wife engaged a cook yet?"

"Why, no, I don't believe she has thought about it."

"Well, I know exactly the woman for her. Elderly, honest, experienced, cooks game to perfection, doesn't drink, thoroughly competent in every way, and the quaintest character I ever knew. Lived in her last place twenty-three years, and only left when the family was broken up. Shall I send her to see you?"

"Do," said Aubrey.

He forgot to tell me about it, so the next morning while he was shaving, a knock came, and in walked Mary. I was in a kimono, writing notes and waiting for breakfast to be sent up. Hearing voices, Aubrey came to the door with one-half of his face covered with lather, and said:

"Oh, yes. I forgot to tell you. Are you the cook sent by Mr. Zanzibar?"

"Yes, sir," said Mary.

Aubrey retired to the bathroom again, communicating with me in pantomime.

I looked at Mary, and loved her. We eyed each other in silence for a moment.

"Won't you sit down?" I said, looking at her white hair.

"Thank you, but I'll stand."

That settled it. I didn't care if she stole the shoes off my feet if she knew her place as well as that. Her face beamed; her skin was fresh and rosy. Her blue eyes twinkled through her spectacles.

"Would you," I said, "would you like to take entire charge of two orphans?"

She burst into a fit of laughter.

"Is it you and your husband, you mean?"

"It is. I wish you would come and keep house for us."

"I'd like to, Missis. I would, indeed."

Again I looked at her and loved her harder.

"Have you any references?" I asked.

"None except the recommendations of the people who have been coming to the house for twenty years. The family are all scattered."

"I have none either," I said. "Shall we take each other on trust?"

"If you are willing," she laughed.

And so we selected each other, and I am just as much flattered as she could possibly be, for neither one so far has given the other notice.

This sketch can only serve to introduce her, as it would take a book to do her justice. She has snow-white hair and a face in which decision and kindness are mingled. She has a tongue which drops blessings and denunciations with equal facility. Born of Irish parents, she belongs to the gentry, yet no fighting Irishman could match her temper when roused, and the Billingsgate which passes through the dumb-waiter between our Mary and the tradespeople is enough to turn the colour of the walls. Yet though I have seen her pull a recreant grocery boy in by his hair, literally by his hair, tradesmen, one and all, adore her, and do errands for her which ought to earn their discharge, and they bring her the pick of the market to avoid having anything less choice thrown in their faces when they come for the next order. She made the ice-man grind coffee for her for a week because he once forgot to come up and put the ice into the refrigerator.

She went among all the tradespeople, and named prices to them which we were to pay if they obtained our valuable patronage. One little man who kept a sort of general store was so impressed by her manner and the awful lies she told about the grandeur of her employers that he presented her with a pitcher in the shape of the figure of Napoleon. Something so very absurd happened in connection with this pitcher some three years later that I particularly remembered the time she got it, and the little man who gave it to her.

She kept house for seven years in Paris, which explains her reverence for food, for we have discovered that the only way to dispose of things is to eat them. Otherwise, in different guises, they return to us until in desperation the Angel sprinkles cigar-ashes over what is left. She pays all the bills and contests her rights to the last penny, once keeping the baker out of his whole bill for five months because he would not recognize her claim for a receipted bill for eight cents which she had paid at the door. As to her relation to us in a social way, those of you who have lived in the South will understand her privileges, when I say that she is a white "Mammy." Her dear old heart is pure gold, and such her quick sympathy that if I want to cry I have to lock myself in my room where she won't see me, for if she sees tears in my eyes she comes and puts her arms around me and weeps, too, without even knowing why, but just with the heavenly pity of one of God's own, although before her eyes are dry she may be damning the butcher in language which curdles the blood.

She abhors profanity, and never mingles holy names in her sentences which contain fluent d's, but being an excellent Catholic enables her to accentuate her remarks with exclamations which she says are prayers; and as these are never denunciatory her theory is most conscientiously lived up to.

In our first housekeeping, our rawness in all matters practical wrung Mary's heart. She had grown up from a slip of a girl in the employ of one family, and ours was only her second experiment in "living out." As her first employers were people of wealth and with half-grown grandchildren when their magnificent home was finally broken up, you can imagine the change to Mary of living with newly married people, engaged in their first struggle with the world. But ours was just the problem which appealed to the motherly heart of our spinster Mary, for she yearned over us with an exceeding great yearning, and of her value to us you your-selves shall be the judge.

The first thing I remember which called my attention to Mary's firm manner of doing business was one day when I was writing letters in the Angel's study. We had only moved in the day before, and the ink on the lease was hardly dry, when I heard a great noise in the kitchen as of moving chairs on a bare floor and Mary's voice raised in fluent denunciation. I flew to the scene and saw a strange man standing on the table with his hands on the electric light metre over the door, while Mary had one hand on his left ankle, and the other on his coat-tails. Her very spectacles were bristling with anger.

"Come down out of that, young feller!" she was crying, jerking both coat-tails and ankle of the unhappy man.

"Leggo my leg!" he retorted.

"*I'll* pull your leg for you," cried Mary, "old woman that I am, more than any of your young jades, if you don't drop that metre. Come down, I say!"

"What is the trouble, Mary?" I asked.

"Missis! The impidence of that brat! He's come to shut off the electric light without a word of warning, and you going to have company this blessed night for dinner."

"Here are my orders," said the man, sullenly. "I'd show them to you if you'd leggo my coat-tails," he added, furiously.

"I'll pull them off before I let go," said Mary, grimly. "A pretty way for the New York Electric Light Company to do business *I* say! If you want a five-dollar deposit from the

Missis why didn't you write and give notice like a Christian? Do you suppose we are thieves? Are we going to loot the house of the electric bulbs, and go and live in splendour on the guilty sales of them?"

"Let me cut it off according to orders, and I'll go to the office and explain, and come back and turn it on for you!" pleaded the man.

But Mary's grasp on leg and coat was firm.

"Not on yer life," she said, derisively. "You'll come back this day week or next month at your own good pleasure, and Mr. Jardine will be doing the explaining and the running to the office. Make up your mind that the thing is going to be settled *my* way, or you'll stay here till you do. *I'm* in no hurry."

"Make her leggo of me," he said to me.

Mary gave me a look, and I obediently turned my back. The man slammed the little door of the metre, and Mary let go of him. He climbed down.

"I can turn it off in the basement just as well," he said, with a grin.

I was about to interfere and offer a cheque, but Mary was too quick for me. She took him by the arm, with a "Come, Missis," and marched him before her, with me meekly following, to the telephone in the Angel's study.

"Now, then, young feller, call up the office!" she commanded. The man obeyed. Indeed few would have dared to resist.

"Now get away and let the Missis talk to your boss. Tell him what we think of such doings, Missis."

I, too, obeyed her. I stated the case in firm language. He apologized, he grovelled. It was all a mistake (Mary sniffed); the man had no such orders (Mary snorted). I could send a cheque at my leisure, and if I would permit him to speak to his henchman all would be well.

I handed the receiver to a very cowed and surly man, whom Mary persistently addressed as "Major." As he turned from the telephone, Mary surveyed him with twinkling eyes.

"Are you going to turn off our electric light, Major?" she said, laughing at him. To my surprise, he laughed with her. Tradespeople always did.

"Not to-day," he said as amiably as though she had been entertaining him at tea. Then she let him out, and went back to her dusting. She looked at me compassionately.

"It's the way that dummed company takes to get people to pay their deposits promptly," she said. "But trust Mary Jane Few Clothes to get ahead of a little trick like that! My, Missis, isn't it hot!"

I went back to my letter-writing feeling somewhat pensive. It was clear that we had a competent person in the kitchen, and as for myself it would not disturb me in the least if she managed me, provided she dealt as peremptorily with the housework as she handled any other difficult proposition. But with the Angel? I was not very well acquainted with my husband myself, and I was slightly exercised as to whether he would bow his neck to Mary's yoke as meekly as I intended to do or not. I seemed to feel intuitively that Mary was a great and gallant general in the domestic field, and my mother's thirty years' war with incompetent servants made me yearn to close my lips as hermetically as an army officer's and blindly obey my general's orders with an unquestioning confidence that the battle would be won by her genius. If it were lost, then it would be my turn to interfere and criticize and show how affairs should have been managed.

But men, as a rule, have no such intuition, and I wondered about the Angel. How little I knew him!

I was arranging the flowers for the table when the Angel came home. When he had gone back to dress, Mary came up to me and in a confidential way said:

"Missis, dear, don't tell your father about the electric light till after dinner,—excuse me for putting in my two cents, but I always was nosey!"

"Tell my father?" I repeated. My father was in Washington.

"Boss! Mr. Jardine!" explained Mary.

"Why did you call him my father? Surely you must know—"

"Pardon me, dear child. I always call him your father when I'm talking to myself, because nobody but your father could be as careful of you as that dear man!"

I sat down to laugh.

"You don't believe much in husbands, then?" I said.

"Saving your presence, that I don't. I believe in fathers, and so I always call that blessed man your father. Will you believe it, Missis, he wouldn't let me reach up to take the globes off to clean them, nor lift the five-gallon water-bottle when it came in full from the grocer. He treats my white hairs as if they were his mother's—God love him!"

I listened to Mary with a dubious mind, divided between admiration of the Angel and the intention of telling him not to help her too much, for fear, after the manner of her kind, she should discover a delicacy of constitution which would prevent her from lifting the water-bottle even when it was empty.

"And I'll tell you what I've been doing on the quiet for him to show him that I'm not ungrateful. You know his white waistcoats have been done up at the laundry so scandalous that I'd not have the face to be taking your money if I were that laundryman, so I've just done them myself, and would you take a look at them before I carry one back for him to put on?"

I took a look, and they were of that faultless order of work that makes you think the millennium has come.

I took one back to where the Angel stood before the mirror wrestling in a speaking silence with his tie. I had not been married long, but I had already learned that there are some moments in a man's life which are not for speech. He smiled at me in the glass to let me know that he recognized my presence, and would attend to me later.

When the tie was made, I drew a long breath.

"The country is saved once more!" I sighed.

He laughed. I mean he smiled. Not once a month does he

laugh, and always then at something which I don't think in the least funny.

As he took the waistcoat from my hand his face lighted up.

"Now that is something like!" he said. "I tell you it pays to complain once in awhile. I wrote that laundry a scorcher about these waistcoats."

"It does pay," I said. Then I explained.

"Do you know what I think?" he said. "I think we've got a regular old cast-iron angel in Mary."

"Oh, rap on wood," I cried, frantically reaching out with both hands. "Do you want her to spill soup down your neck tonight?"

"I didn't think," he said, apologetically, groping for wood. "*Now*, do I dare speak?"

"Yes, go on. What do you think of her?"

"I think she is thoroughly competent to deal with the emergencies of a New York apartment-house. This morning just before I went out I heard her holding a heart-to-heart talk with the grocer. It seems that the eggs come in boxes done up in pink cotton and laid by patent hens that stamp their owner's name on each egg. For the privilege of eating these delicacies we pay the Paris price for eggs. Now it would also seem that these hens guarantee at that price to lay and deliver to the purchaser an unbroken, uncracked, wholly perfect egg in the first flush of its youth. But to-day the careless hens had delivered two cracked eggs out of one unhappy dozen to Mary. With a directness of address seldom met with in good society, Mary thus delivered herself down the dumb-waiter,

'Well, damn you for a groceryman—'"

"Oh, Aubrey! Did she say that word?"

"She said just that. 'When we are paying a dollar a look at eggs, what do you mean by sending me two cracked ones out of twelve? To be sure *somebody* has been sitting on these eggs, but I'll swear it wasn't a hen.' His reply was inaudible, but he was just going out to his wagon, and he was opening up his heart to the butcher boy as I passed. 'I'd give five dollars, poor as I am,' he said, 'for one look at that old woman's face, for she talks for all the world just like my own mother.' And with that he exchanged the two cracked eggs for two perfect ones out of another order, and took the good ones in to Mary."

"I wonder if it will last," I said to a woman who was envying the fact that I could persuade Aubrey to go out with me whenever I wanted him to.

"It *won't* last!" she declared, cheerfully. "And it won't last that Mr. Jardine will go calling with you evenings. The clubs will claim him within six months, and as for Mary—I'll tell you what I'll do. I'll wager you a ten-pound box of candy that within a year you will have lost both your husband and your cook."

"Lost my husband," I cried, my face stiffening.

"Oh, I only mean as we all lose our husbands," she explained, airily. "I used to have Jack, but I am married now to golf links and the club."

"I'll take your bet," I said.

"You'll lose," she laughed. "They are both too perfect

to last."

"They are not!" I cried.

But when the door closed, I rapped on wood.

# CHAPTER II

## THEORIES

If there is anything more delightful than to furnish one's first home, I have yet to discover it. Aubrey says that "moving in goes it one better," but his preference is based on the solid satisfaction he takes in putting in two shelves where one grew before and in providing towel-racks and closet-hooks wherever there is an inviting wall-space for them.

But to me, even the list I made out and changed and figured on and priced before I made a single purchase was full of possibilities, and contained wild flutters of excitement on account of certain innovations I wished to try.

"Aubrey," I said one evening as the Angel sat reading Draper's "Intellectual Development of Europe," "have you any pet theories?"

"What's that? Pet theories about what?"

"Housekeeping."

"I don't quite understand. I've never kept house, you know."

"I mean did your mother keep her house and buy her

furniture and manage her servants to suit you, or exactly as you would do if you had been in her place?"

"Not in the least," said the Angel, laying down his book, all interest at once.

"Ah! I knew it! Then you *have* theories! That's what I wanted to bring out. Now I have theories, too. One is the rag-bag theory."

"The—?"

"The theory that every housewife must have a rag-bag. My mother had one because her mother did and *her* mother because *hers* did, and so on back to the English one who probably brought *her* rag-bag across with her. Ours was made of bed-ticking, and had a draw-string in it and hung in the bathroom closet. Now if you ever tried to lift a heavy bag down from a hook and knew the bother of emptying it of neat little rolls of every sort of cloth from big rolls of cotton-batting to little bundles of silk patches and having to look through every one of them to find a scrap of white taffeta to line a stock, then you know what a trial of temper the family rag-bag is."

"And you—" said the Angel, who is definite in his conclusions.

"*I* mean to have a large drawer in a good light absolutely *sacrificed*, as some people would call it, to the scraps. When you want a rag or a bone or a hank of hair in our house, all you will have to do is to pull out an easy sliding drawer without opening a door that sticks, or crawling into a dark corner, or having to light a candle, or doing anything to ruffle your temper or your hair. A flood of brilliant sunlight or moonlight will pour into my rag-drawer, and a few pawings of your unoccupied hand will bring everything to the top. Won't that be joyful?"

Aubrey, who loves to fuss about repairs and is for ever wanting material, was so enchanted with the picture I drew that he longed to have a cut finger to bind up on the spot.

"Have you any more theories?" he asked, laying Draper on his knee without even marking his place.

"A few. Some are about buying furniture."

"We want everything good," said Aubrey, firmly.

"More than that. We want *some* things beautiful. And some things *very* expensive."

I thought I saw the bank-book give a nervous flop just here. But perhaps it was only Aubrey's expression of countenance which changed.

"For instance, I want no chairs for show. Every spot intended to rest the human frame in our house shall bring a sigh of relief from the weary one who sinks into it. I have already started it by the couch I ordered last week for your study. I went to the man who takes orders and said: 'Have you ever read "Trilby"?' And he said no, but his wife had when it was the rage about five years ago. I had brought a copy on purpose, so I read him that paragraph from the first chapter describing the studio. Here it is: 'An immense divan spread itself in width and length and delightful thickness just beneath the big north window, the business window—a divan so immense that three well-fed, well-contented Englishmen could all lie lazily smoking their pipes on it at once, without being in each other's way, and very often did!' He smiled and said it made very agreeable reading, to which

I replied that I wanted one made just like it."

"What did he say?"

"Well, of course he argued. He wanted to make it a normal size. He wanted to know the size of the doors it would have to go through, and I told him it was for an apartment. As soon as he knew that he wanted to make the lower part of cedar to store furs in for the winter. I said: 'No, no! This is a luxury. There is to be nothing useful about it. I want the whole inside given up to springs!' He said, 'Turkish?' and I said yes, and put in two sets of them. At that he began to catch the spirit of the thing and took an interest. We argued so over the size of it that finally I told him to send out and measure the elevator and the door and the room it was to go in and make it just as large as those spaces would allow. So you'll have a divan ten by six. I wanted it bigger, but I couldn't have got it through any front door."

"Why, won't it about fill that little room?" asked my husband, with a trace of anxiety in his tone.

"Only about half-way. There's just room for a little table of books at one end of the divan, and I'm going to have a movable electric lamp with a ground-glass globe and a green shade to be good for the eyes. Your pipe-rack will be on the wall over it. Then by squeezing a little there will be just room for my writing-chair,—you know the one with the desk on the arm and the little drawer for note-paper?"

Aubrey got up and came over to where I had my list, and Draper fell to the floor unnoticed.

"I never heard anything sound so comfortable," he said. The Angel is always appreciative, and, moreover, is never too absorbed or too tired to express it fluently. That's one of the things which make it such a pleasure to plan his comfort.

"Doesn't it sound winter evening-y and snowy outside?" I said.

"I can hear the wind howling," said the Angel. "What's the next item?"

"Well, now we come to a theory. Of course I have had no more experience than you in buying furniture, but it stands to reason that some of the things we buy now will be with us at death. Some furniture stays by you like a murder. For instance, a dining-room table. I have known some very rich people in my life, Aubrey, but I have seldom seen any who grew rich gradually who had had the moral courage to discard a dining-room table if it were even decently good. Have you ever thought about that?"

"I can't say that I have, but it is fraught with possibility. 'The Ethics of Household Furniture' would make good reading."

"Well, haven't you," I persisted, "in all seriousness, haven't you seen some very handsome modern dining-rooms marred by a dinner-table too good to throw away, which you were convinced the family had begun housekeeping with?"

"Yes, I have!" cried Aubrey. "You are right, I have. I thought you were jesting at first."

"Well, I am, sort of half-way. But the sort of dinner-table I want to buy is no joke. It is one which will grace an apartment or a palace. We can be proud of it even when we are rich. Yet it is not showy, or one which will be too screamingly prominent. It is of carved oak with the value all in the carving. It costs—" Here I whispered the price, for to us it was almost a crime to think of it.

The Angel looked sober when my whisper reached him. But he did not commit himself. I eyed him anxiously.

"But to make up for that outlay, here is the way I have planned the rest of the house. Let's have no drawing-room."

"No drawing-room? Then where will you receive guests?"

"The room will be there, and people may come into it and sit down, but it will not be familiar ground to strangers. They will find themselves in a cheerful room with soothing walls and comfortable chairs. There will be books and magazines. It will not be a library, for quantities of bookcases discourage the frivolous. It will have no gilt chairs, because big men always want to sit in them. It will have no lace curtains, because I hate them. The piano will be there and most of our wedding-presents,—all which lend themselves to the decoration of a room which will look as if people lived in it."

"If you put bric-a-brac in it people will call it a parlour in spite of you," said the Angel.

"Not at all. It will have one distinguishing feature which will effectually prevent the discriminating from making that mistake. I intend to make the clock on the mantel *go*. That will settle matters."

"Of course."

"This room will lack the stiffness of a drawing-room and so invite conversation, yet will be sufficiently dignified to prevent familiarity. I shall endeavour to invest it with an invitation which will practically say to your college friends, 'You may smoke here, but you may not throw ashes on the floor.' Do you see my point?"

The Angel looked thoughtful.

"I hope it will work," he said.

"We can but try it. I am doing this because I wish our friends to meet us together, and I don't approve of this separating men and women,—the women remaining alone to gossip while the men go away to smoke. It is too narrowing on us and too broadening on you."

"I like it,—in theory,—but some men are chimneys. They don't know how to smoke when ladies are present."

"They will soon learn!" I declared, stoutly. "I shall be so attentive to their comfort, so ready with an ash-tray, so eager to offer them the last cigar in the jar (if I think they have smoked enough) that they will notice my slightest cough."

Aubrey waxed enthusiastic.

"An evening spent in that room will be 'An Education in Polite Smoking,' won't it?"

"And," I went on, "then when we are rich and want a truly handsome drawingroom we can furnish it in pink silk and cupids with a light heart, for behold, we will simply move all this comfort I have described into a library, and the wear on the furniture will redeem it from newness and give it the proper air of age and use. There is nothing more vulgar to my mind than a perfectly new library. It looks—well, you know!"

"It does," said the Angel, with conviction. "All of that!"

We discussed these theories in detail, made many corrections, and finally went down to buy. But a handsome shop and money in my pocket always excite me so that what little common sense I was born with instantly departs, and I buy feverishly, mostly things I do not want and could not use. So the Angel adopted a good, safe rule. When he saw my eyes begin to glitter with a "I-must-have-that-or-die" expression, he used to take me by the arm and say:

"Now shut your eyes, and I'll get you past this counter."

I have heard of many curious women who do not enjoy housekeeping. I am free to confess that I do not understand why, unless they started out in life with the conceited idea that to bend their wonderful brains upon the silly problem of keeping a house clean and ordering dinners was beneath women of their possibilities on club essays. I often wonder if they attacked the proposition of housekeeping with the intention of seeing how much fun there is in it, of how much pleasure could be got out of making a home, not merely keeping house, and of feeding their conceit with the fuel of a determination to keep house better than any woman of their acquaintance. The simple but fascinating problem of how to make each room a little prettier than it was last week, would keep even an ingenious woman busy and interested in something worth while, and those of us who are sensitive to impressions would be spared the truly awful sight of certain incongruous rooms in handsome houses. Oh, if you only knew what people say about you—you women who "don't like to keep house!"

But I forgot. Most women have no sense of humour, and few husbands take the intense interest in a home that the Angel does.

America, foreigners claim, is a country almost as homeless as France is said to be. The French have no word for home in their language, but they have homes in fact, which is much more worth while. We Americans have the lovely word "Home," but we haven't as a nation the article in fact. Americans have houses, but in truth we are a homeless race. Only the unenlightened will contradict me for saying that, and for the opinion of the unenlightened I do not care.

I am not sentimental after the fashion of women who send flowers to murderers, but I am full of pale and sickly theories as to the making of a home, and I am free to confess that it would give me more pleasure to hear people say of me, "Mrs. Jardine's husband is the happiest man I know," than to have them read on a bronze tablet under a statue in the Louvre, "Faith Jardine, Sculptor." For if more ambitious women would devote themselves to making one neglected husband happy the public would be spared weak and indifferent pictures, silly and rank books, rainy-day skirts in the house, and heaps of other foolishness and bad taste, most of which at bottom is not the necessity to work for a living, but simply Feminine Conceit.

Of course Aubrey and I made some mistakes in spite of all our precautions, for, happily for me, the Angel can be led away by enthusiasm, and is not so faultlessly perfect as to be impossible to get on with. I revel in his weaknesses, they are so human and companionable, and give me such a feeling of satisfaction when summing up my own faults. We got so much fun out of shopping for the house that we dragged out the process to make the delight of it as lingering as possible. I had planned it all out.

My own room was to be pink. Big pink roses splashed all over the cretonne counterpane and valance of the bed. Plain pink wall-paper upon which to hang pictures all in black frames. Small pink roses tumbling on the ceiling and looking as if every moment they would scatter their curling petals on the pink rugs on the floor. The dark furniture against the pink walls toned down the rose colour, which returned the compliment to the furniture by bringing out the carving on bold relief.

The guest-room, on the contrary, was to be pale blue with white furniture. Nothing but gold-framed pictures on the walls and a blue rug on the floor. The chairs were to be upholstered in blue for this room, and in pink for mine. Muslin curtains with full deep ruffles, picked out respectively with pink and blue, would flutter at the sunny windows, and though simplicity itself, nothing ever struck me as any more attractive, for it was all mine—my first house—my first housekeeping! When this dream really came true, I walked around in such a dazed condition of delight that I was black and blue from knocking myself into things I didn't see. But even as I did not see the obstructions, I did not feel the pain of my bruises, for they were all got from my furniture on corners of *my* house, and thus were sacred.

As I gazed on the delicate beauty of my pretty little guest-chamber I fell to wondering who would be its first occupant. Would it be a man or a woman? Would it be Artie Beguelin, the Angel's best man, or my sweet friend and bridesmaid, Cary Farquhar?

At any rate, he or she would be welcome—oh, so welcome! I hoped the invisible guest would be happy, and would feel that ours was not a compulsory hospitality, with the cost counted beforehand and the benefits we expected in return discounted. No, whoever it was to be would be a guest and a friend. On the wall over the bed hung these words illuminated on vellum and framed, for I had always loved them:

"Sleep sweet, within this quiet room,
Oh thou, whoe'er thou art!
And let no mournful yesterday

Disturb thy peaceful heart,
Nor let to-morrow fret thy dreams
With thoughts of coming ill,
Thy Maker is thy changeless Friend,
His love surrounds thee still.
Sleep sweet!
Good night."

Afterward, when my first guest had come and gone, this momentary reverie came back to me, and I looked up at this benediction with tears in my eyes.

Of course we spent too much money on our house furnishings. We always do, but after all—and here come my theories again. I would have fine table and bed linen. The Angel did not believe I would stick to it, but I did embroider it all myself. And as to hemming napkins and table-cloths—I challenge any nun in any convent to make prettier French hems than I put in! Would I be likely to waste all that labour on flimsy napkins or cotton sheets and pillow-cases?

Not at all! I can find infinitely more pleasure in putting invisible stitches into my own first linen than in going to pink teas, and people don't get permanently angry if you invite them to dinner, and let them eat off hemmed and embroidered damask. Believe me. You may send cards to six receptions, and get out of six afternoons of misery and indigestion by one judiciously arranged dinner—if you don't mix your people. And thus we did.

So I got my linen. The Angel laughed at another of my theories, but when I proved to him that I would really see the thing through, he was convinced. It was on the question of beds. Our friends professed themselves astonished that we contemplated the extravagance of a guest-chamber, for here in New York, where rents are so abnormal, people economize first of all upon their friends, and I am told that an extra bedroom where a chance guest may be asked to remain overnight is the exception with people of moderate means. Such monstrous selfishness struck me as appalling. To provide *only* for ourselves—for our own comfort! To have no room in all your own luxury to share with a friend! To be obliged to tell the woman whose hospitality you have enjoyed in your girlhood: "Now that I am married, I have prepared no place for you! Your kindness to me is all forgotten!"

Well, we simply refused. What if it were a strain on us financially? I would rather suffer that than cripple myself spiritually and suffer from no pangs of conscience as most New Yorkers do!

However, we managed it, and in this wise. I said:

"Aubrey, if you are willing, we can save a great deal in this way."

Even at this early stage the Angel always grew deeply attentive when I talked of saving anything.

"We can and must order the finest springs and mattresses for the beds, for of all the meanness in this world the meanest is to put a bad bed in the guest-chamber, and that is where most housekeepers are perfectly willing to economize. But we can and will buy white iron beds with brass trimmings for almost nothing,—they are all the same size as the fine brass ones,— so that at any time when we find ourselves vulgarly rich and able to live up to the dinner-table we shall feel perfectly justified in discarding them, and there you are!"

"But how will it look?" said the man.

"How will our bank-account look, if we don't?"

"I know. But I thought women were afraid of what other women would say," said the Angel.

"Now, Aubrey," I said, "If we have economized on ourselves, or rather included ourselves in a general scheme of economy in order the better to provide for our guests, I think even New Yorkers would hesitate to criticize the Jardines' iron beds,—especially if they ever got a chance to disport themselves on the Jardines' Turkish springs!"

"There's something in that," said the Angel.

# CHAPTER III

## ON THE SUBJECT OF JANITORS

I used to pride myself on being practical and on possessing no small degree of that peculiar brand of sense known as "horse." However, like most women inclined to take a rosy view of their virtues and to pass lightly over their obvious faults, I know now that I prided myself on the one thing in my make-up conspicuous by its absence. For I am luxurious to a degree, and so fond of beauty and grace that I feel with the man who said, "Give me the luxuries of life and I will do without the necessities."

This explanation is due to any man, woman, or child who has ever lived in a New York apartment, and who is moved to follow the fortunes of the Jardines further. Also this conversation took place before some of the events already narrated transpired, and while we were still at the Waldorf.

"Now, Aubrey," I said, "to begin at the beginning, marriage is supposed to perfect existence all around, isn't it?"

"It does," said Aubrey.

"No, now, I am speaking seriously. It has fed the mental and spiritual side of us, why not begin life with the determination to make it oil the wheels of daily existence? Why not bend our energies to avoiding the pitfalls of the ordinary mortal, and let *us* lead a perfect life."

"Very well," said the Angel.

"Now in permitting housekeeping to conquer, most people become slaves to the small ills of life, which I wish to avoid."

"Get to the point," said Aubrey, encouragingly, fearing, I suppose, that if he did not give the conversation a fillip, I might go on in that strain for ever, which would be wearing.

"Well, the point is this. I've never known what it was to have good service in a private house, except abroad. Now even when people bring excellent servants over from London and Paris, they go all to pieces in a year. It's in the air of America."

"Well?" said Aubrey.

"Well, of course we have perfect service here in this hotel, and it seems to me that the nearest approach to that would be in one of those smart apartment-houses, where everything is done for you outside of your four walls. Then with Mary, who seems to be a delightful creature, all we need do is to be careful in the selection of a janitor. Do you follow me?"

"You have not finished," said Solomon.

"Quite true, oh, wise man of the East! Another of the trials of my life has always been to get letters mailed."

"To get letters *mailed*?" said Aubrey.

"To get letters mailed," I repeated, firmly. "Every woman knows that it is no trouble to write them, but the problem of leaving them on the hall-table for the first person who goes out to mail, the lingering fear when one doesn't hear promptly that the letter was lost or never went; the danger of somebody covering them up with papers and sweeping them off to be burned; the impossibility of running to the box with each one; the impoliteness of refusing the friend who offers to mail them permission even to touch them,—oh, Aubrey, really, the chief worry of my whole life has been to get letters mailed!"

"The most expensive apartment we looked at had a mail-chute," said my husband, thoughtfully, after a moment of silence.

"Well," I hazarded, timidly, "the only difference between a flat and an apartment is in the rent."

"That apartment had an ice-box and a sideboard built in, and a mail chute," repeated Aubrey.

"Yes, it did, as well as the most respectful janitor I ever saw. Did you notice him?"

"Was he the one who was cross-eyed?"

"Well, yes, I think his eyes weren't quite straight. But that may have been one reason why he was so gentle and deferential. I have often noticed that persons who are afflicted in some painful way are often the very kindest and best, as if the spiritual had developed at the expense of the physical."

"Well, Faith, if your heart is set on that one we must have it."

"I know the rent is exorbitant, but I intend to get all of my amusement and recreation out of my home, so count balls and receptions and functions out—or rather count them in the rent," I said, "for instead of going to the theatre as we have been doing, I want to give little dinners—real dinners to people we love, and give them with a view to the enjoyment of our guests rather than that of ourselves. I want to make a fine art of the selection of guests in their relation to each other."

"I'd like nothing better," declared Aubrey, "but don't you know that you won't be called upon to do much of that sort of thing the first winter, for everybody we know will be entertaining us."

"There's one other point I'd like to explain," I said. "And that is that I shall never entertain anybody whom I simply 'feel called upon' to entertain, nor, if I like people, shall I count favours with them. I shall conform to conventionality simply as a matter of dignity. It is the privilege of your friends to make the first advances to me because I am a stranger to most of them. But I want to make a practice of hospitality for my own sake. I want to see if the open house we kept in the South cannot be accomplished in New York. I never, for the good of my own soul, want to grow as cold and calculating as some so-called hospitable women whom I have met in the North."

Aubrey looked at me comprehendingly.

"I know," I said, smiling, "that it sounds to a hardened New Yorker like yourself about like the interview of a young actress who declares that she intends to elevate the stage. But in my case, I am in the position of one who doesn't want the stage to lower her. I don't want to grow cold, Aubrey, and I hope never to allow a friend to leave my house at meal-time without at least an invitation to remain and make, if necessary, a convenience of us. What are friends for, I should like to know?"

"From the position you have just stated I should think your definition of a friend would be 'a man or woman who can be imposed upon with impunity.'"

"Let them impose upon me if they want to," I declared, stoutly. "As long as I have respectful service, I will let those I love make a door-mat of me!"

"A slightly volcanic door-mat, I should say," observed the Angel. "You would allow yourself to be stamped upon just about as humbly as a charge of dynamite, and the remonstrance in both cases would be similar."

I could not help remembering this conversation after we had moved in and we had been settled by the efforts of the family of the cross-eyed janitor.

I never enjoyed anything in my life as I enjoyed moving into our first home. It was on the top floor, overlooking the park from the front windows, while the back gave upon a stretch of neat little flower gardens with the Hudson shining like a narrow silver ribbon between us and the undulating Jersey shore.

Every room was light. Every room opened on the street, and the sunlight came pouring in quite as if it did not know that in most apartments the sun is an unexpected luxury. There were parquet floors throughout, and the bathroom was white marble, all except a narrow frieze of cool pale green. The woodwork was daintily carved, the dining-room was panelled in oak with two handsome china-closets built in. We had eleven closets with an extra storeroom for trunks in the basement, and enough cabinets in the kitchen and butler's pantry to stock a hotel, and as a crowning glory the front door did not open opposite the bathroom or kitchen as is the case in most apartments, but was near the front like the home of a Christian, and the dining-room gave into the front room with a largeness of vista which made us feel like millionaires.

Does this read like a fairy-tale?

As we surveyed our domain, I felt such a flood of gratitude and pride of home sweep over my soul that I said to Aubrey:

"I actually feel like praying."

The Angel smiled an inscrutable smile, the exact meaning of which I did not catch, but it was not one of derision. Rather I should say that it had in it a waiting quality, as of a knowing one who intended to give thanks after he had tested a meal, instead of a reckless wight who in faith called down a blessing on a napkin and salt-cellars. But my gratitude was largely "a lively appreciation of favours to come."

I have no tale of woe to relate of things which did not come in time. Our purchases promised for a certain day arrived as scheduled, were uncrated on the sidewalk, with Aubrey and me hanging out of the sixth floor window to watch them. The gentle-mannered janitor and his buxom daughter were cleaning the last of the windows, and such was the genius of fortune and Mary that at three that same afternoon, when the best man called to see how we were getting on, there was nothing left to do but to hang pictures, so we set him to doing that while we sat around in languid delight and bossed the job. But it was thirsty work, and the best man rested often. Such perfection of planning seemed to irritate him, although he is by nature a gentle soul, for he said, "I must say you have done well, but I'll bet there is one thing you have forgotten."

"Not at all," said Aubrey, who was at college with the best man. "There are six siphons on the ice now, and six more under the kitchen sink. The corkscrew is on the mantel."

All the pictures were hung before dinner. That is, they were hung for the first time. The pictures in our apartment have travelled. One by one they have journeyed from the smoking-room down the long hall, stopping a day or two in each room, and all finding a resting-place except one, which will not look well in any colour, any spot, on any wall, nor in any light. It was a wedding-present from some one we like, or Aubrey would have put his foot through it long ago. As it is, it is under the blue room bed, whence we drag it every once in awhile to admire the frame and say, "I wonder if it wouldn't go there."

As long as that picture remains unhung, a vacant wall space in any house is full of interest and possibility to us, and if we ever move, we shall select a spot for that picture first, and consider the rent and plumbing second.

The janitor's manners continued perfect. Even Mary found no fault with him, and as my appreciation for anything is plainly evident in my manner, both Mary and the janitor felt that in me they had found a friend, and they waxed confidential withal.

One day he came up to clean windows, and when he mentioned the "parlour," I said:

"Don't call this room a parlour. I have neither parlour nor drawing-room. This small room is a smoking-room, and this other is a library. I wanted Mr. Jardine to feel at liberty to smoke all over the house."

The janitor looked about him and noticed the lack of gilt chairs and lace curtains.

"Will you excuse an old man for speaking, Mrs. Jardine, and not think me impertinent if I make free to say that if more young ladies started housekeeping with such ideas, homes would be happier. I make bold to say that you will not have trouble in keeping Mr. Jardine at home evenings."

I blushed with pleasure at having won the approval of this gentle soul. But when I told Aubrey he said:

"Poor old fellow! I saw his wife to-day. She weighs well on to four hundred, and has the air of an anarchist queen. She was engaged in reducing the agent to his proper level, and *I* fled."

Evidently the agent conquered, for, alas! within a week we had a new janitor,—the opposite of my friend in every respect. Harris, the new janitor, was young, sprightly, self-confident, and an American of the type "I'm just as good as you are." This challenge lay so plainly in his eye that almost involuntarily I said, "I know you are," before I told him that the elevator squeaked.

I hated him from the moment I saw him, but I gave him an extra large fee to bribe, in the cowardly manner of all citizens of the land of the free and the home of the brave, a servant to do pleasantly the duties he is otherwise paid to do. He had three little children, and when one of them had a birthday I sent them ice-cream and a birthday cake. When his wife fell ill I sent her my own doctor, for her little pale, pinched, three-cornered face appealed to me. She did all the janitor's work. It was her voice at the dumb-waiter instead of his, and once Aubrey found her emptying a garbage can nearly as large as she was, when he went down to see why Harris didn't answer our bell. Aubrey found Harris asleep.

We discovered these things by degrees, and gradually I came to feel that my mail-chute was the only real, continuous luxury we had gained with this awful rent. Still we avoided discussing the matter. By ignoring it, we could keep ourselves deceived a little longer to the fact that we were being robbed by our own foolishness.

One day I invited the dearest old lady, over ninety years old, to luncheon. Her daughter was to bring her in her carriage, and I made Aubrey promise to be in the house by eleven o'clock in case she needed assistance, and I prepared to have a beautiful day. For weeks we had planned for this festival, for it was Mrs. Scofield's ninety-first birthday and would probably be her only outing during the winter. At ten o'clock I had word that she felt well enough to come, so I told Aubrey to bring over the ninety-one roses he had ordered in honour of her birthday.

He came in looking a florist shop. We arranged them, and waited and waited and waited. At two o'clock, the most disappointed of mortals, we sat down to luncheon.

"I am afraid something has happened," I said, and the anxiety and disappointment threw me into such a headache that I spent the afternoon in a darkened room, and had tea and toast sent in for my dinner.

About eight o'clock Aubrey persuaded me to go out for a little walk, so we started. We had no sooner got outside our door than we began to feel impending calamity in the air. The elevator was not running. There was a paper saying so fastened to the bell. We walked down five flights of stairs, occasionally looking at each other ominously. My headache vanished as if by magic. I felt strong and murderous.

On the table in the hall lay a dozen letters, which had arrived during the day, a telegram from Uncle John, asking us to dine at the Waldorf and share their box to see Irving and Terry and to sup with them at Sherry's that night. It was then a quarter to nine. We were not dressed, and we were half an hour from the theatre. There was also a note from Mrs. Scofield's daughter saying that they had come at half-past twelve, but found no hall-boy, no janitor, and the elevator not running, so, after vainly trying to communicate with us, they had been obliged to go home again.

I simply wept with rage and mortification. Aubrey started for the basement with me at his heels. I felt that the Angel could not cope alone with such a situation. We found Mrs. Harris pale, trembling, and apologetic. She said her husband was not there.

Aubrey turned away breathing vengeance.

"Aubrey," I said, firmly, "Harris is in that room."

"No, no, Mrs. Jardine! Indeed he is not!" insisted the little woman.

"I am sorry for you, Mrs. Harris," I said, "but you must allow me to see for myself." And with that I made as if to pass her, but Aubrey held me back.

"I'll go," he said.

He went and found Harris calmly reading the newspaper, with his feet on the mantel.

"Why isn't the elevator running?" demanded Aubrey.

"Because the hall-boy left this morning, and there was nobody to run it," said the man, impudently keeping his seat, with his hat on, and not even putting his feet on the floor.

"Is it broken?" asked my husband.

"It is not. I turned the power off, that's all."

"Why didn't you run it yourself?" asked Aubrey.

"It isn't my business. That's why, young feller. Now you know, don't you!"

"Don't you dare speak to my husband in that manner," I broke in. Aubrey shook his head at me. It was cruel of him, for I do love a fight.

"You come out this minute and start that elevator," said Aubrcy.

"I'll do nothing of the sort. You'll walk up those five nights of stairs this night," said the janitor. Oh, how I wished I had that fee back!

Mrs. Harris plucked imploringly at my skirt.

"Harris, aren't you ashamed of yourself?" I said. "Look at your poor wife just out of bed, and you have lost this good place by this day's work. You and your family will not know where to lay your heads within a week."

"And how do you know that? I'll keep this place as long as I please. *I* stand in with the agent. I suppose you think because you've been good to the children that you can run me, but let me tell you that you've not done half that you should! So you just shut up and go back where you belong."

Aubrey made a leap for him, but Mrs. Harris threw herself between them and I fastened myself to Aubrey's coat-tails. This was more than I had bargained for.

"No, Aubrey, come. Let us once for all declare our independence. For some time I have suspected that there was collusion between janitors and agents. Now let's get to the bottom of it."

By holding out such a prospect to him, I got the Angel upstairs, where we poured forth our souls in a letter to the agent.

He called, listened to us with polite incredulity, and said he would hear Harris's side, as if he wished to judge impartially between two criminals.

We held on to ourselves while he consulted the gentleman below stairs. When he came back he said:

"Harris denies everything. Now who am I to believe?"

For once the Angel rose to the occasion.

"Mr. Jepson, you may believe whom you please if you have no more decency than to put the word of a gentleman against that of a drunken servant. You have violated the terms of our lease, and unless Harris is dismissed inside of a week our apartment is at your disposal."

"Very well, Mr. Jardine," said Jepson, "if you insist on our dismissing a janitor for his first offence without even giving him a second chance, then there is nothing to do but to agree to your demand."

Aubrey bowed in a truly haughty manner. The Angel!

"I so insist," he said. The agent left us.

"Aubrey," I said, thoughtfully, "we have gained a gallant victory over the janitor, but I fear the battle with the agent will be the bloodiest of our campaign."

But we looked forward hopefully. Like all man-eating monsters, having once tasted human blood, we thirsted for more.

# CHAPTER IV

## THE ANGEL AND THE AGENT

At the risk of causing the gentle reader to despise us, I feel in duty bound to set forth the joys and sorrows of our first housekeeping about as they occurred. By that I mean that I intend to take the keen edge from our griefs for kindness' sake and to illuminate our joys a little beyond the stern realities as we found them, in order to permit the reader to understand the colour of the Paradise that the Angel and I found in each other. If, therefore, I do not burst into tears at the moment when any well-regulated woman would, lay it, O gentle reader, at the door of the Angel, whose deep-seeing understanding not only could comprehend such a grief as that of parting with my dog, but which also was capable of sympathizing with suitable violence over a gown which did not fit or the polite malice of an afternoon visitor.

If I add that when I went into a fury over nothing at all the Angel never attempted to stop me or to pooh-pooh the cause, but permitted me to mangle the whole subject until it lay a disorganized, dismembered, wholly unrecognizable mass at my triumphant feet, I feel reasonably sure that I shall have proved to every woman his right to his title.

The knowing ones will naturally scorn the method of

reasoning by which we arrived at conclusions, but I have found that nothing is more diverting or delightful than to go blundering into absurd predicaments, mentally hand in hand, for the Angel never says "I told you so." That sting being removed and all three in this happy family, Mary, the Angel, and I, all being rather handsomely endowed with a sense of humour, it is a constant source of enjoyment to look back and consider the virulence and contagion of our ignorance and to count the bruises by which we became wise.

One evening at ten o'clock we came in from making a call and found the elevator-boy in his shirt-sleeves washing the hall floor. I asked him if it wasn't a little early to be doing such a thing, as people were still going and coming, and he said he was acting under Mr. Jepson's orders. Jepson was the agent.

We said we would remonstrate, and we wrote a letter to Jepson asking him to have the hall cleaned after twelve o'clock at night and before six o'clock in the morning. He wrote back that, after consulting the convenience of all the people in the house, he had decided on eight in the morning and ten at night, as everybody was at breakfast at the first hour and that ten was the freest hour for the halls at night. He added that the gentleman on the first floor went fishing at six every morning, and had complained of having the halls washed at that hour, as he was inconvenienced thereby.

A few days later we met Jepson on the street, and Aubrey stopped him and said:

"There are several matters about the house I wish you would look into, Mr. Jepson."

"Now look here, Mr. Jardine, if you expect me to run that whole apartment-house to suit you, you are going to be mistaken."

"For whose comfort and convenience is it run?" I broke in before Aubrey could stop me.

"For mine, madam! I arrange everything outside of your four walls."

"Then we have no rights as to entrance, elevator, and our upper hall?" asked Aubrey.

"None, sir!"

I pulled the Angel away.

"Now, Aubrey," I said, "*I* have had an apartment in Paris, and I know what the power of the concierge is. But if you think for one minute that I am going to submit to such impertinence here in America, you never were more mistaken in your life."

"What do you intend to do?" asked my husband, with the very natural and perfectly excusable interest a man takes when he sees his wife donning her war-paint.

"The trouble with me is that I am too agreeable," I went on, firmly. The Angel never flinched even at that statement. "I am too polite. We ask for our rights as if we were requesting favours."

"Is it our right to say when the halls shall be cleaned?" asked Aubrey.

"Well, I leave it to you as a business man. There is a difference of eight hundred dollars a year in the rent between the first floor and ours. If we pay the highest rent shouldn't our wishes be considered first?"

"Eight hundred dollars' worth first!" agreed Aubrey.

"Well, now I'll tell you what I think we would better do, and see if you don't agree with me. To tell the truth, I am getting a little sick of the tyranny of agents and janitors, and I propose to see if by making a firm stand we cannot establish a precedent for the rights of tenants."

"Don't go to law," said Aubrey, "for every law in New York State seems to favour agents and janitors. I've conducted too many cases not to know."

"We won't go to law. We will use common sense. It vexes me to hear everybody telling what abuses they stand in New York apartments, and not one of them has the courage to make a fight for liberty. An Englishman wouldn't stand it for one minute, but we Americans are cowards about 'scenes' and 'fusses' and such things, and year by year our rights are passing from our hands into the hands of foreigners and the lower classes, who already rule us because they don't mind a fight."

"True," said Aubrey.

Much flattered by his approval, I proceeded more calmly. It always puts me in a heavenly temper not to be opposed.

"Now we will give this Jepson person one more chance. If he abuses his authority or tramples on even the fringe of our rights, we will revolt."

"Good!" cried Aubrey, perfectly willing to become enthusiastic over an encounter not in the immediate future. But his peaceful disposition once roused, and my inflammable nature crawls into the darkest corner under the bed to escape the sight of the consequences.

It came to be the first week in October without anything more irritating happening than that all our protests had been disregarded, and we picked our way through sloppy halls and dismissed our guests with forced jests about bathing suits being furnished by the agent for them to reach the street door in safety, and all such things, keeping up a proud front, but secretly mortified almost to death, for anybody would know from our location that we were paying a high rent, and then to think—

However—

On this early October morning we found frost on the windows, and, although we had no thermometer, we knew that we were cold. We hurried out into the dining-room and lighted the gas-logs. They were new, and inside of five minutes we had every window in the house open and handkerchiefs to our noses. We said we would stand it and burn the new off, but we have lived here two years and the new is still on. So then we said we must have heat. This was before Janitor Harris left, so Aubrey, after ringing in vain for half an hour, went down and told him to make a fire in the furnaces. Harris said we were to have no heat until the fifteenth of November. It was a rule of all apartment-houses. Aubrey said, "Nonsense!" But when he came up-stairs Mary confirmed the janitor. She said it was a rule in New York.

We said nothing, but we felt that this was the time for our declaration of independence.

First we bought thermometers for every room.

Then Aubrey looked up the law.

In all the bedrooms the mercury stayed at forty-nine until noon, then it got to fifty-one. At seven that night it dropped to forty-five, and in the morning all the windows were frosted again.

Aubrey's law partner was extremely interested in all our plans, for he also lived in an apartment and wanted heat, but knew better than to ask for it. Our lease was so worded that we were to have "heat when necessary." Our rights hung upon when the agent, who was five miles away, or the owner, who was in Florida, should agree upon how cold we were to be allowed to grow before thawing us out. Then, carefully planning the campaign, Aubrey wrote letters and had interviews with the agent, in which he committed himself in the presence of witnesses and on paper until, on the afternoon of the third day of our cold storage, Aubrey wrote to the agent saying that if we did not have heat within twenty-four hours, we should go to a hotel and stay until they chose to give it to us, and take it out of the rent. This letter evidently tickled one of the clerks in the agent's office to such an extent that he called Aubrey up by telephone and said he had done the only thing possible under the circumstances to bring the company to book. This approval pleased Aubrey, and he asked the man's name. It was Brooks.

We all felt that Brooks was a gentleman.

"They will *never* let us do *that*, Aubrey," I said.

"They will think we are bluffing!" said the Angel, with quiet conviction.

"Bluffing!" I cried. "Do they think we won't go if they don't give us heat?"

"They little know *you*, do they?" said Aubrey, patting the

sleeve of my sealskin, for I wore it all day now. I put it on when I got up.

We waited the twenty-four hours, and then as no notice had been taken of our letter we calmly packed a handbag, bade Mary good-bye,—she had the gas range to keep warm by,— and much to her delight we went down to the Waldorf. But not to our old luxurious quarters. We took a room and a bath at five dollars a day. We were doing this from stern principle, and we wanted a reasonable case.

I have never flattered myself privately that I am a particularly agreeable woman, but I can truthfully say that we were extremely popular at the Waldorf, for in some manner it had leaked out that we were making a test case on the "heat before the 15th," and everybody we knew who lived in apartments called to see if we were really there, and some who didn't know us sent word to us or walked by to look at us, as if we were performing animals. The name of Jardine was paged through the corridors and billiard-room and cafe until we had a personal acquaintance with every menial in the hotel. It cost us a good deal to get away, I remember.

All these first-mentioned nice persons encouraged us, and slapped Aubrey on the back and called him "old chap," much to his annoyance (for the Angel hates familiarity from chance acquaintances), and said we were doing the right thing and God-blessed-us and wanted us to promise to let them know how we came out.

We said nothing, but we could see that not one among them all but expected either a lawsuit or that we would be obliged to back down and pay for this foolhardy defiance of the despot out of our own pockets.

Each day we went out to the apartment and examined the

thermometers and took signed statements as to the degree they registered. We had notified the agent that we would not return until it was sixty-eight Fahrenheit in the bedrooms.

On the afternoon of the third day the weather had moderated to such an extent that it was sixty-eight, so I stayed while Aubrey went down to the Waldorf for the bill and our bag. On his return he proudly exhibited a receipted bill for $27.

As no reply had been received to our letter and no one had been sent to see us, we felt a truly justifiable pride in the little surprise we had for Jepson when on the first of November the Angel sent a cheque for November rent, less $27, together with the now famous receipted bill.

If we felt that we had been ignored by our agent hitherto, we had no cause for complaint after the receipt of that bill and cheque. In fact, as I told Aubrey, Jepson did not have time to use a paper-knife on the envelope,—he must have torn it open with feverish fingers,—for the telephone-bell jingled madly before breakfast when the office "wanted to know the meaning of this," and when the Angel rang off without any reply, poor old Jepson came up to the apartment out of breath.

We got plenty of attention after *that*!

Jepson was at first quite confident—even patronizing.

"Why, don't you know, Mr. Jardine, we can't allow any such absurd thing as this to go on—not for a minute."

"Ah," said Aubrey. "What do you propose to do about it?"

"I propose to leave this—this—er—bill and cheque with you and collect the full amount of the rent."

"I don't envy you the process," said my husband.

"Oh, well, I imagine there will be no trouble about it. We know our rights."

"Has it ever occurred to you that we might know ours?" said Aubrey.

"Yes, certainly. But you know, Mr. Jardine, we are agents for a large number of the best apartment-houses in New York, and we have not given heat to any one so far."

"I only live in this one," said Aubrey. "It does not interest me in the least what temperature other of your tenants prefer. I shall have this apartment warm when *I* think it is cold."

"Well, but—I understand how you feel, but—no one ever did such a thing as this before in the whole course of my thirty-five years' experience."

"I can quite believe it," said Aubrey, thinking of the people we knew who suffered without a protest.

"Then you can imagine my surprise this morning to receive this," said Jepson.

"I can quite imagine it," returned my husband, with an irony wasted on Jepson, but delightful to me.

"Well," said our visitor, rising, "I hope you will think better of it and send me a cheque for the full amount. It will save unpleasantness."

"I anticipate unpleasantness from my past experience with you," said the Angel, "and that is every cent you will get from me for November rent."

Lilian Bell

"Then we shall sue you, Mr. Jardine. Doubtless you would be embarrassed to be sued for twenty-seven dollars."

"It wouldn't embarrass me to be sued for twenty-seven cents," said Aubrey, cheerfully, for he always expands in good nature when the other man shows signs of temper.

"Do you expect us to sue?" asked the astonished agent.

"Here is my defence," said Aubrey, pleasantly, drawing a bundle of law papers from his pocket. "My partner and I have been at work on this case for a fortnight."

Jepson sat down again suddenly and unwound his neck-scarf. The Angel does look gentle.

"I didn't think—" he began and stopped, but Aubrey helped him out.

"You didn't think several things, Mr. Jepson. You didn't think I meant it when I said I must have heat. You didn't think I meant it when I wrote you that I would go to a hotel if you didn't give it to me. You didn't think I would resent your paying no attention to our requests about cleaning the halls. You didn't think I intended to live in this apartment to suit my own comfort and convenience and not yours. You didn't think I could force you to live up to the terms of our lease, which says 'heat when necessary.' But I intend to give you an opportunity right now to change your mind about several things."

Jepson dropped his hat on the floor and fumbled for it.

"I'll take the matter up with the president of our company," he said.

"Do," said Aubrey, cordially.

The next morning while Aubrey was down-town the president of the real estate company called.

"Now, Mrs. Jardine," he said, "I just thought I would drop in while your husband was away to discuss this little difficulty in a friendly way and see if you and I couldn't come to some arrangement by which both parties will be satisfied."

"Yes?" I said.

"You see, Mrs. Jardine, you as a lady will realize that your husband took a very high-handed way,—in fact, I may say it was the most high-handed proceeding I have ever heard of in all my business career."

"Yes? I suppose it must have astonished you as much as it amazed us to discover that we were to be heated by date instead of by temperature."

"Er—er well! Of course, you didn't know, but you must understand that that rule obtains among all agents in New York."

"So we heard," I said, indifferently.

"You know that?"

"Oh, certainly."

"Did you know what method Mr. Jardine was about to pursue to force us to heat your apartment before any one else asked for heat?"

"I suggested it to him," I said, gently.

"You sug—Well, of course. Hum! I see."

"And as for none of the other tenants wanting heat, every family in the house asked for it. The lady on the third floor has a five-weeks-old baby, and, as you know, there are no gas-logs in any of the bedrooms."

"Well," said the president, rising, "I must look into this. I will take the matter up with the owners."

"Good morning," I said. "I will tell Mr. Jardine that you called."

"Yes, do," he said, hurriedly putting on his hat, and then taking it off again. "Good morning. Mr. Jardine will hear from me."

"I hope so," I said to myself as Mary closed the door. "We never have before."

The owners called next, singly and in couples. We were delighted to meet them, for we were convinced that we never would have had the pleasure of their acquaintance under any other circumstances.

After more interviews and letters than any $27 ever occasioned before, we finally received a letter stating that our claim had been allowed, and they enclosed a receipt in full for November's rent.

Nobody believed us when we told them, and we nearly wore the letter out exhibiting it. It is worn at the folding places now from much handling, like an autograph letter of Lincoln's or Washington's.

During the following year a new firm of agents took

possession of us, who knew us not, so that the next October, when we wanted heat, the same patronizing manner greeted the Angel when he telephoned for permission to have the janitor light the furnaces.

"Oh, no. Oh, no, Mr.—er—Really, we couldn't consider such a request," came a voice.

"Look here," said Aubrey. "I am the man who went to the Waldorf last year when the agent refused us heat and took twenty-seven dollars out of the rent. You may have heard of me."

"What name, sir? Oh, Jardine! Yes, Mr. Jardine, you shall have heat within an hour."

The next morning the janitor—also a new one by the way— told the Angel that he got a telephone message from the agent to start a fire in the furnace if he had to tear off wooden doors and burn them!

"All of which goes to show," said Aubrey to me, "that some-body ought to write a book on 'The Value of the Kicker.'"

# CHAPTER V

## HOW WE TAMED THE COOK

Second only to the skill required in managing a husband is the diplomacy necessary in the art of living with one's cook. Therefore let the unmarried pass this over, feeling that the time for them to read it is not yet, but let those who have a cross-grained, crotchety, obstinate, or bad-tempered cook take this to a quiet corner and hear my tale. While it may not be exactly your experience it cannot fail to touch a responsive chord, for whether you have already had a spoiled cook or not, rest assured that you will have one some day, and do not scorn to make her the subject of deep and earnest study and the object of diplomatic negotiations.

In our case Mary was old and obstinate, but her virtues were too many to dismiss her without valiant efforts made to reform her in one or two particulars. It is, alas! but too true, that perfection does not exist, especially in cooks. But as even her failings leaned to virtue's side we bore and bore with her, making light of our inconveniences, and pretending not to notice that we could never make her do anything that she had not wanted to do beforehand. It was a good deal of a strain on us sometimes, for we are self-respecting folk, with excellent opinions of ourselves.

But among her good points was an absolute reverence for food. She never wasted a mouthful, even saving the crusts she cut from the toast to grind for breading and doing all the thrifty things one would do oneself, but which no cook ever born is expected to do nowadays. She had lived some years in Paris, for one thing, and for another,—"Missis, I always believe that them that wastes—wants. I've seen it too many times to want to run the risk."

Mary is a character, but this theory of hers she carried to an extreme, as you shall hear.

Owing to our respect for Mary's white hairs, the dinner-hour was as changeable as a weathercock. We dined anywhere from seven to nine, and soothed each other's irritation by calling ostentatious attention to the delicacy and perfection of each dish as it came on the table. Why shouldn't each be perfect, forsooth, when no amount of coaxing or persuading, no amount of instructions beforehand or hints or orders could make that cook of ours lift a finger toward dinner until we both were in the house with hungry countenances and expectant demeanours? We even tried telephoning her from down-town that we were on the way and would be at home in an hour. When we came in at the end of that hour and said:

"Mary, is dinner ready?" the answer was always:

"No, dear child, but it will be in a minute."

At first we believed her and hurried to get ready, but as ten, twenty, thirty minutes passed and no signs of soup appeared, we used to take turns strolling carelessly into the kitchen as if to see what time it was, to investigate the progress of dinner. If we came in at seven we got it at eight. There was no way apparently of circumventing her. She would have her own way.

Once the Angel said:

"Mary, didn't we telephone you that we wanted dinner just as soon as we came in?"

"Yes, sir!"

"Well, wasn't it six o'clock when we telephoned?"

"Yes, sir, but I just thought maybe you would be delayed or the car would run off the track or you'd stop to talk to some friends, so I wouldn't begin to cook until I clapped my two eyes on you."

At first we used to laugh and say that it was her respect for food. Then it worked on our tempers and grew anything but funny. It got to be exasperating, infuriating, maddening.

"Now, Aubrey," I said, "it has come to the battle with the cook. Shall we submit to petty tyranny or shall we strike?"

"I'll tell you what," said the Angel. "I haven't quite made up my mind whether Mary is really amenable to kindness or whether she takes us for suckers."

"Oh," I gasped. I had never taken myself for a "sucker" before, and even in such good company as that of my husband it gave me a jar to hear the possibility mentioned.

"I am convinced of one thing," he went on, "Mary has been badly spoiled, and, while I have no objection to her ruling us in any way she likes, I am going to compel her to obey orders when she gets them."

"Oh, be careful!" I cried.

"I'm going to. But first I am going to investigate the labyrinths of her mind. If it is that she respects food more than she does our feelings, I'll do one thing. If it is that kindness won't work, I'll try severity. But I'm going to make that old woman obey me and have dinner on time."

The Angel delivered this alarming ultimatum without raising his voice and with no more emphasis than he would use in saying:

"May I trouble you for the salt?"

I leaned back and looked at him.

"As if you could be severe with any one, you Angel!"

From which remark the knowing can easily deduce the length of time we had been married.

It was then ten minutes to eight. We had come in at six, and at five we had telephoned her to have dinner promptly at seven.

"I hope you had a good tea," said Aubrey, looking at the clock.

"I did. It isn't that I am hungry. I'm mad," I answered, genially.

"I am not mad. I am hungry," said Aubrey.

"Being hungry for a man is the same as being mad for a woman," I observed.

Aubrey grinned.

"Now," he said, mysteriously. "Don't eat any dinner to-night, and follow my lead in everything."

"Don't eat any dinner!" I cried, in a whisper. "I am starv—"

"Hush," he whispered. "You said you weren't hungry."

Although we were only ten feet away from her and in plain view, Mary struck the Roman chime of bells, by which she always announces dinner.

As we took our seats the clock struck eight. The table was a dream of loveliness. Wedding-silver, wedding-glass, wedding-linen graced it at every turn, for Mary always decorates for us as for a banquet.

Never has the fragrant odour of soup assailed me as it did on that particular night. Mary hovered around, watching to see how we liked it. We tasted it, and laid our spoons down. We talked languidly, without noticing her.

"What's the matter with the soup?" she finally demanded when she could stand it no longer. We looked up as if surprised.

"Why, nothing," said Aubrey. "I don't care for it. That's all. Take it away."

"It will do nicely for to-morrow night," said Mary.

At that Aubrey dropped his entire cigarette into his and I put a spoonful of salt into mine.

"Isn't it good, Missis?" asked Mary of me.

"I don't know," I said, wearily. "I'm too tired to eat."

"Take it away," said Aubrey again.

"My poor dear child!" cried Mary. "Too tired to eat! But eating will do you good. Taste a bit! Try it, Missis dear!"

"No, I don't seem to care for it, and I was very hungry at seven o'clock. Don't you remember, Aubrey, I said coming up in the elevator how hungry I was?"

"I remember," said my husband. "But you are just like me. If you don't have your meals at a certain time your appetite goes."

At that Mary lifted her head and looked at us through her spectacles. Never were four more innocent eyes to be met with than ours. We looked at her calmly until she lowered her gaze. It was not an impudent nor a defiant look she gave us. It was a trial of wills. Our two against her one.

She removed the soup without more ado, and brought in a broiled chicken. Oh, oh! Shall I ever forget it! I was so hungry by that time that I could have bitten a piece out of my plate.

Mary stood by with a face as anxious as if she were standing by the death-bed of her child.

Aubrey lifted it with the carving-fork, looked at me, and said:

"Do you feel as if you could eat a little bit of this?"

A little bit! I felt as if I could have snatched it in my paws and run growling to a corner to devour the whole of it and to bury the bones for the next day.

"No," I said, wearily, leaning my head on my hand to hide my countenance. "But you eat some, dear."

Aubrey laid down the carving-fork.

"No, I don't care for any."

"What time did you have your luncheon, dear?" I asked, anxiously.

"At half-past twelve. I had an appointment with Squires at one."

"And what did you have?" I continued, for Mary's face was expressive of the liveliest horror.

"A club sandwich and a glass of beer."

Mary looked at the clock. It was half-past eight.

"Oh, my dear!" I said, mournfully. "It is no wonder you can't eat. Your stomach is too exhausted to feel hunger."

Mary ran around the table for no reason at all. She took the cover off the best silver dish. It was a dish of fresh peas cooked with onions and lettuce. Petits pois a la paysanne! I had taught her myself! I simply glared at it. To this day I can smell those onions!

"If I could have had those at seven o'clock," said Aubrey, sadly, "I could have eaten every one of them. They look delicious, Mary, but I really—no, don't urge me! Take the dinner off."

"Oh, boss dear, if you'd just take a lick at them!" implored Mary. "Just one lick—there's a handsome man!"

Aubrey bit his lips. I was trembling on the verge of hysterical laughter.

Mary implored in vain. With our famished eyes on the peas and chicken we saw them disappear through the swinging door. Mary in her agony was talking aloud.

"Keep it up!" whispered the Angel. "This will fetch her! She's ready to cry."

"Oh, but Aubrey," I moaned. "I'm ready to gnaw the napkin and eat my slippers. Please come and tighten my belt!"

"I know now how explorers and castaways feel," murmured the Angel. "For heaven's sake, what comes next?"

"Asparagus!" I wailed. "Fresh asparagus. I paid ninety cents for it! And she's cooked it with her white sauce—oh!"

The door opened and Mary, with pink cheeks and dancing eyes, brought in and deposited before me my favourite dish. Asparagus on toast. I looked at it longingly, feverishly! I was famishing. My throat was dry and my eyes had a savage glare. I had heard of men going mad for want of food. I know now how they felt.

At first I could not speak. I was obliged to swallow violently.

"There!" cried Mary, triumphantly. "You can't pass that up!"

"Alas!" I sighed, shaking my head. I looked at her and felt simply murderous. That white-haired old woman's obstinacy in not giving us our dinner on time was the cause of all my misery. I resolved to rub it in. Her face was a study.

"Did you ever," I said, mournfully, "see me refuse asparagus before?"

"You're never going to refuse it!" exclaimed Mary, incredulously. "Missis! I used a pint of cream, to say nothing of the butter! Why, it's a sin! It's a mortal sin in you not to try it! See, Missis, let me put a little on your plate. I'll feed it to you like as if you were a baby! I will indeed!"

"No," I said, clutching at the table-cloth to keep from falling upon that dish of asparagus and shovelling it down my throat in huge handfuls,—"no, I couldn't! Mary! I am too weak, really, I think I am starving!"

I leaned back and closed my eyes. The clock struck nine.

"You've had nothing to eat all day!" cried Mary. "You had only a bite for your lunch, and that was eight hours ago! Oh, Missis, dear! Ain't I the mean dog! Let me make you a cup of tea! Missis dear! In the name of God eat something! Do!"

"No," I said. "I have always been this way. If I go five minutes over the time when I expect my dinner, I feel just this way. I can't eat."

With which astonishing lie, I leaned back as if death were already looming up in the distance.

Mary made one more attack. Salad was the Angel's weak point as asparagus was mine, and Mary always made a dream of beauty out of it. She scorned "*fatiguer la laitue*" as the French do. Instead she kept it in a bowl of water until thoroughly "awake," as she called it. Then carefully examining each leaf separately, she tied them in a wet cloth and laid them "spang on the ice," which course of treatment rendered them so crisp that to cut them with a sharp salad-fork was always to get a little dressing splashed in one's eye. Furthermore she arranged them in the best cut-glass dish in symmetrical rows with the scarlet tomatoes tucked invitingly in the centre. She presented us with such a dish on this evening. Then when Aubrey (who will be remembered when he is no more, not for his moral qualities nor for his domestic virtues, but for the skill with which he used to mix a salad dressing) went to work and prepared one from tarragon, vinegar, oil, Nepaul pepper, paprika, black and cayenne pepper, to say nothing of plenty of salt,—words fail me! I simply pass away at the recollection.

I have never been able to make up my mind whether Mary suspected us or not. Of course we overdid the part, but it was a physical necessity. I can go without a thing altogether, but I cannot be moderate. I really thought I was not hungry until Aubrey told me not to eat, and that, of course, was enough to make any woman ravenous. If he had told me "to buck up and eat a good dinner," of course I could only have nibbled.

She broke out again, and pleaded hard for us to drink our coffee, but we were obdurate.

Finally we got up from the table and Mary removed the cloth, muttering to herself. I overheard some of it, but where any other cook would have been furious at us for not eating her delicious dinner, the dear old soul's rage was all directed against herself, and she was vituperating herself in language which would not have gone through the mails.

But now the question was where and how to get our dinner so that Mary would not suspect. To send her to church and forage in our own ice-box was out of the question, for she knows to a dot how much there is of everything, and I cannot take an olive that she does not miss it and come and ask me if I took it, to avert suspicion from the ice-man. Furthermore, it we both went out, she might suspect. And we had taught her too heroic a lesson to go and spoil it by carelessness now.

"What shall we do?" murmured my husband.

"There's only one thing to do," I said, in low, even tones, with my book before my face. "Go out and buy something ready cooked,—something which leaves no trace,—something small enough to go into your overcoat pocket, but oh, in the name of heaven, get enough!"

Mary came in as the outer door slammed.

"Where's boss gone?" she demanded. Perhaps it was only my guilty conscience which made her tones sound suspicious.

"Just over to Columbus Avenue to get a paper," I said.

"Oh!"

I waited in a guilty and trembling silence for the Angel to return. What if Mary should take it into her head to come and help him off with his overcoat? She often did. I softly opened the outer door. If she didn't hear him enter, all would be well.

Presently he came up. He got out of the elevator stealthily, and I met him with my finger on my lip.

"Aren't you going to take off your hat?" I said, as he stole down the corridor.

"Can't!" he whispered. "I've got cream puffs in it."

I only waited to ward off an attack from the rear. I put my head in at the butler's pantry.

"Mary, I have such a headache that I am going to bed now, so be as quiet as you can, won't you?"

"I'll come and open the bed for you right this instantaneous minute, my poor dear child," she said, taking her hands out of the dish-water.

"No, I'll open it! I don't mind in the least," I said, eagerly.

"Not at all! Do you think I'll be letting you lift your hand when you're sick?"

Finding that I could not prevent her, I hurried down the hall to discover the Angel looking wildly for a place of escape— still with his hat on. I motioned him into the bathroom, and his coat-tails disappeared therein, just as Mary loomed into view.

It took her a full quarter of an hour to open that bed, for nothing would do but she must unhook me. And all that time my thoughts were on the cream puffs. I did hope that Aubrey would have sense enough to put them on the wash-stand.

Finally I got rid of Mary, and released the Angel. He clanked as he came in, but that was two pint bottles of beer.

I locked the door, and then he unloaded. Besides the beer and cream puffs, he had four devilled crabs and two dill pickles, four club sandwiches, some Roquefort cheese, and some Bent biscuits.

He was obliged to make one more dangerous pilgrimage to the front hall to slam the door and hang up his hat and coat, otherwise Mary would have gone out after him. We have such a competent cook.

Finally we sat down and gorged on that impossible mixture. We had only Aubrey's pocket-knife, a paper-cutter, and a button-hook to eat with, and rather than to stop and wash out his shaving-cup we drank out of the bottles.

We ate until we felt the need of dyspepsia tablets, but still there was some left. This Aubrey did up in a neat package, we raised the window, turned out the lights, and threw it far, far out into the night. We listened and heard it fall in a neighbour's back yard.

Now, if we had stopped there, all would have been well, but Fate tempted us in the person of a vile and nasty little curly white dog, with a pink skin and a blue ribbon around her neck, whose mistress used to lead her up and down in front of our apartment-house every evening. She was a very nasty little dog, badly spoiled, and we had longed to kick her for six months, but her mistress was always there and we couldn't.

But oh, joy! On this particular night, she was in the back yard all alone, yapping and whining to get indoors. Clearly this was the best place for the empty beer bottles.

"Don't hit her, Aubrey. Just aim for the cement walk. That will scare her to death."

The Angel seldom follows my wicked counsel, but this was the hand of Providence. No one, who has not owned a big dog, can know how we hated this miserable, pampered little cur.

So Aubrey took aim. The beer bottle hurtled through the air.

We stepped back and listened. It crashed on the walk, and such a series of agonized yelps from the frightened little beast resulted as I never before had heard. We clutched each other in silent ecstasy. Fortunately the pup's mistress had not heard.

Emboldened by success we stole forth again, and shied the second bottle. But that time Providence was against us, for, at the identical moment that the bottle hit the corner of the house and flew into a million pieces, the door opened and the dog's mistress appeared.

The crash was something awful. Nobody was hit or hurt, but the woman shrieked and the Angel and I fell to the floor as if shot. Instantly windows flew up, and as each head appeared the infuriated woman accused it of having thrown the bottle. I reached for the Angel's hand as we grovelled on the floor, and our former spirit returned as indignant denials were followed by more indignant slamming of windows.

Finally—silence. Two hands sneaked up in the darkness and pulled our window down.

"We could prove an alibi," I giggled, "for Mary would go on the stand and swear that I was in bed prostrated with a headache!"

The next night the soup was on the table at five minutes before seven, and we heard that the white dog was laid up for a week with an "*attaque des nerfs*."

"Who would have thought," I sighed, in delight, "of the luck of fetching Mary and that white dog both in one evening!"

# CHAPTER VI

## THE BEST MAN'S STORY

Trouble began to brew for the best man at my bridesmaid's dinner, but it was all his fault. He says it was mine.

I claim, and I think that all girls will support me in this theory, that at all wedding functions, such as teas, receptions, luncheons, and dinners, the best man owes the maid of honour the first and most of his attentions. It is her due, and no matter whether he likes her or hates her; no matter if he is already in love with another girl, or sees one there that he would like to be in love with, he belongs, for the wedding festivities, to the first bridesmaid. It is like the girl your hostess assigns to you at dinner,—you *must* be nice to her.

So Cary Farquhar thought, and so I think. Artie Beguelin said:

"Then you oughtn't to have invited Flora Forsyth to the bridesmaid's dinner."

Well, perhaps I oughtn't. But I did, because she asked to come. One can't refuse a request of that sort. Even Aubrey admits that.

Flora was a dreamy, trusting blonde. She was an innocent appearing little thing, and although she was just out of college, I believed she would faint at the idea of a cigarette in a girl's fingers or any of the mad things college girls are supposed to do when larking. She had no sense of humour, and I simply could not think of her as up to any mischief. That is why, when she said she had fallen in love with me, I believed her. She knew I was to have Cary for my only attendant, but she begged so innocently to come to the bridesmaid's dinner and to sit with the family behind the white ribbon, that I hadn't the heart to say no. That is why she was at the dinner, and what happened there you shall hear presently.

Arthur Beguelin was the Angel's best man. He, too, was Aubrey's sole attendant, for we had no ushers.

Artie was neither clever nor stupid, but that gentle, amiable cross between the two which made him fair game for a designing girl. He was better than clever. He was magnetic, as Cary and Flora found to their sorrow.

His father had been enormously wealthy, but his vast property had slipped out of his keeping, and had become involved in a lawsuit of such dimensions and such hopeless duration that Artie might just as well consider himself as a ward in chancery, and be done with it.

This loss of fortune, however, instead of demoralizing him, had been his salvation. It set him to work, and made a man of him. He never believed that he would inherit a dollar of his father's, so he prepared to make his own way in the world, regardless of golden hopes.

But not so his friends. His prospects, hazy as they were, made him most interesting to match-making mothers, and as his indomitable courage made him interesting to the other and better sort, you will see that Artie was pursued rather more than most eligible young men. This pursuit had made him wary and cautious. Had he been more introspective, it would have embittered him; but it shows his amiable modesty when I assert that Artie only fought shy of the more aggressive anglers, whose landing-nets were always in evidence, while he never refused to swim nimbly around and even nibble at the bait of the more tactful.

I have described him thus carefully, because it just shows how the most wary of men can be caught napping by the right kind of cleverness, and which was the right girl for him it took both us and him some time to discover.

At first sight, it seemed to be Flora. As Aubrey said: "It was all off with him from the moment he saw her." He had been the stroke in the Yale crew during two glorious years of victory, and, like most men who gloried in the companionship of athletic girls, he elected to fall in love with Flora, who, the first time she met him, wanted to know the difference between a putter and a bunker, which so tickled Artie that he put in two good hours explaining it to her.

Cary had known Flora for some time, but two girls could not have been more unlike. Cary was rich, courted, and flattered. She had only to express a wish to have it granted, yet, strange anomaly, she was the most unselfish girl I ever knew, and was always going out of her way to be nice to people.

Flora was poor. She went to college by means of a loan from a rich woman, and kept herself there by winning scholarships. She expected to teach for a living, and she hated the prospect. She had to work hard for everything she had, which was probably the reason why she was so selfish. To be sure, she was always offering you things, but it was either after some one else had offered first, or else she offered things you couldn't possibly want. And as to offering to do things for you, I never saw her equal at the formula, "I am going down-town. Can't I do something for you?" Yet if you by any chance made the mistake of saying, "That's awfully good of you. I *would* like three yards of French nainsook," in half an hour Flora would come in with the story that she had been telephoned out to luncheon and wasn't going down-town, or else had a headache and couldn't go, after all; or, if she went, she did her own shopping first and came in breathless with a "I'm so tired! I went everywhere for your French nainsook, but every shop was just out of it. I tried *so* hard, and now you'll think I am just stupid and *can't* shop."

At which you always had to comfort her and do something extra for her, to show that you didn't blame her in the least. Whenever she had grossly imposed upon you, Flora had a way of looking at you with what I called the "dog look,"—a humble, faithful, adoring, "don't-kick-me-because-I-love-you-so" look, which used to give me what Angel calls the jiggle-jaggles, which is only another name for twitching nerves,—either mental or physical.

However, I have noticed that these people who are always offering their "Can't I do something for you?" never expect to be taken up. I suppose it isn't in human nature any more to be helpful to a friend. The answer to that question is "Thank you so much, dear, for offering, but I really don't want a thing!" That cements the friendship.

Cary was honest, straightforward, and thoughtful. Flora was crafty, deceitful, and brilliant, but her innocent eyes and baby ways made her cleverness seem like that of a precocious child, so that she always disarmed suspicion.

She deceived me so skilfully and completely that I find myself thoroughly mixed in describing her, for at one moment I tell how she appeared to me at first, and the next I find myself setting her forth as I found her after Cary and Aubrey had set a trap to make me see her in her true light. They were obliged to set a trap, for my loyalty is of the blind, stupid sort, which will not be convinced, and all the arguments in the world would only have made me more ardently champion her as a friend.

You could not call Cary athletic, because she did not go in for out-of-door sports to the exclusion of the gentler forms of amusement. But whatever she did, she did so well that you would think she had given most of her time to the mastering of that one accomplishment. But here is where her cleverness showed most. It was not that she really did everything, and did it perfectly. It was that she never attempted anything which she had not mastered. For example, she never played whist, because she had no memory, no finesse, and because she played games of chance so much better. She could never settle herself down to a multitude of details, but she could plan and execute a coup of such brilliancy that it would make your hair stand on end. Such was Cary Farquhar, and her most successful coup was the way she compelled me to see Flora Forsyth in her true colours.

Sometimes I think I am quite clever. Again I think I am a perfect fool. And the agains come oftener than the sometimes.

I would enjoy making a continuous narrative of this story, as I could if I were writing a book, but this is a record of real life, and real life does not happen in finished chapters. If you try to make it, you either have to leave out a bit, or go back and repeat something.

Thus, in telling this story of Flora, if I told the perfect faith I had in her at first and of how utterly I came to know and despise her afterward, I should show to everybody the fool I made of myself, and that exhibition I prefer to keep as much to myself as possible. The Angel knows it, and that is bad enough. So that is why I must make a hodge-podge of it, telling a bit here and a bit there, just as things happened, and pretending that I saw through her from the first—which, however, I didn't.

But, in order to give some idea of her methods, which are of interest as a human document, I must set down faithfully how I came to be drawn into this love-story, and how the Angel and Cary pulled me out.

This is the very beginning of it.

If you knew our best man, you probably would not be surprised to make the discovery that I made—to wit: that two girls were in love with him at the same time, for the most ordinary of men have sometimes a powerful attraction for the most superior of girls, and Arthur Beguelin was much above the ordinary, in looks, manners, breeding, and wealth. He was, as I have said, almost rich, which would of itself, to the cynic, preclude his being at all nice. But he was nice. I liked him, the Angel liked him, and these two girls loved him.

I will admit, however, that I was surprised,—just a little,—at first, but after I thought about it, I said to Aubrey, "Well, why not?" He said, "Why not what?"

"Why *shouldn't* two girls be in love with him?"

"They should," said the Angel, pleasantly. "There is no doubt in the world that they should. But who are the girls and who is the man?"

I thought of course that he knew what I was talking about, or I shouldn't have begun in the middle like that, but after all, if you *do* begin in the middle, you can often skip the whole beginning, and hurry along to the end.

"Why, Artie Beg, to be sure! Who else? And as to the girls—well, as I discovered it for myself, I shall not be betraying their confidence to say that the girls are—will you *promise* not to tell nor to interfere in anyway?"

"Of course," said the Angel.

"Well, the girls are Flora Forsyth and Cary Farquhar."

"Flora Forsyth!" exclaimed the Angel, with a wry face.

"Now, Aubrey, what *have* you against that poor girl? To me she is one of the most fascinating creatures I ever saw. If I were a man, I should be crazy about her."

"Then if you had been Samson, Delilah would have made a fool of you just as easily as she did of him."

"But Flora is no Delilah, Aubrey."

"She's worse!" said the Angel, shortly.

Aubrey leaned back in his Morris chair and puffed at his pipe. Presently he spoke:

"Those two girls are both clever,—as clever as they make 'em,—but Cary's cleverness is full of ozone, while Flora's is permeated with a narcotic. Cary's tricks make one laugh, but the other girl's give one the shivers."

"Oh, is it as bad as that?" I said, in affright. "Don't you

like her?"

"Like her!" reflected the Angel, slowly. "I hate her."

I gasped. Never, never had my husband expressed even a settled dislike of any one before, while as to the word "hate"—

"Oh, Aubrey!" I cried, tearfully. "I *wish* you had said it before. The fact is, I've—well, I've invited her to visit me and she says she'll come."

If I expected an explosion, I was mistaken. Aubrey bit into his pipe-stem and sat looking at me for a moment without speaking, a kind, wistful look which completely undid me, and made me resolved never, *never* again to do a single thing without consulting him first. Then he leaned forward and slowly began to empty and clean his pipe.

"You like her very much?" he said, tentatively.

"I do, indeed!" I exclaimed, enthusiastically. "And she is *so* fond of you. She fairly adores you. If you would only *try* to like her, Aubrey—she likes you so much—don't smile that way. You don't do her justice. Indeed you don't. Why, she is the dearest, most confiding, innocent little thing, just out of college last month—a baby couldn't have more clinging, dependent ways."

"I'm glad she is coming to visit you, if that's the way you feel about her," he said.

I drew a sigh of relief. *Some* husbands would have made such a fuss that their wives would have felt obliged to cancel the invitation. Aubrey was different.

"How did you come to invite her?" he asked, presently.

I smiled in pleased anticipation of a good long talk with my husband, in which I could explain everything.

"Why, you know at the wedding I saw that Artie was very much taken with her,—and—"

"First, tell me how she came to sit with the family, inside the white ribbon?"

"Why, she wrote and asked if she couldn't. She said she loved me so she felt as if she were losing a sister, and that she wanted to sit with mother and mourn with the family."

Aubrey grinned and I felt foolish.

"And you believed her, you silly little cat!"

"It does sound idiotic to repeat it, but it read as if she meant it," I said, blushing.

"Never mind, dear," said the Angel. "You are all right."

Now, when Aubrey says I am "all right," it means that I am all wrong, but that he loves me in spite of it.

"Bee says," I said between laughing and crying, "that I am just like a stray dog. A pat on the head and a few kind words, and I'd follow anybody off."

"It would take something more substantial than that to make Bee follow anybody off," observed Bee's brother-in-law.

"Well, and so she and he were together all that evening, and afterward they corresponded. But Cary, being my bridesmaid, had, of course, the first claim on Artie's attention, but he was so taken with Flora that he sort of neglected Cary. Then, Cary being so spoiled by being rich and courted and flattered, was piqued into trying to make him notice her, which old stupid Artie refused to do, but tagged around after Flora as if she had hypnotized him. Then Cary must have been quite roused, for the first thing I knew she was showing unmistakable signs of its being the real thing with her, though, of course, she would deny it with oaths if I taxed her, while Flora—"

I stopped in sudden confusion.

"I forget," I faltered. "I said that neither had confided in me, but—"

Aubrey grinned.

"But Flora has," he supplemented. "She has confessed her love, not blushingly, but tumultuously, brazenly, tempestuously, and has begged you to help her!"

I paused aghast. Aubrey had exactly stated the case.

"Well, she told Cary, too," I said, in self-extenuation, "so she can't care very much that I've told you."

"Oh, no," said Aubrey, cheerfully. "She'll tell me herself the first chance she gets."

"She told Cary that she had told me, so we felt at liberty to talk it over," I added.

"She did?"

"And Cary was perfectly disgusted with her, and asked  what

I was going to do. I said I didn't know. Then what do you think she did? Cary asked me to ask Flora to visit me! What do you think of that for a bluff?"

Again Aubrey grinned. He shook his head.

"That was no bluff, Faith dear. That was a move in a game of chess. Cary Farquhar is the choicest—*unmarried*—girl I know! By Jove, she's a corker!"

"She just did it to throw me off—to show me that *she* didn't want him!" I persisted.

The Angel shook his head and smiled inscrutably.

"When does she come?" he asked.

"Next week."

Aubrey pulled at his pipe.

"There will be something doing here next week, I'm thinking."

There was something doing.

First, I told old Mary that I was going to have company.

One ordinarily does not ask permission of one's cook, but Mary was such a mother to me that I felt the announcement to be no more than her due.

"Who is it, Missus, dear?"

"Miss Flora Forsyth. Have you ever heard me speak of her?"

"Do you mean that blonde on the mantelpiece?" she asked, in the conversational tone of one who but passed the time o' day.

"Mary!" I said.

She walked up to Flora's picture, took it down, looked at it, and put it back.

"Well," I said, tentatively, "what do you think of her?"

"What do I think of her?" demanded Mary, wheeling on me so suddenly that I dodged. "I think she is a little blister— that's what I think of her. And you'll rue the day you ever asked her into your house."

Ordinarily one would reprove one's cook for such freedom of speech, but I had brought it on myself. Therefore I saved my breath, put on my hat, and went out, ruminating and somewhat shaken in my mind to have the two household authorities against me.

However, true to my determination to make her visit as attractive as possible, I purchased at least a dozen sorts of fine French marmalades, jellies, sweets, and fancy pickles, such as schoolgirls love.

She had told me so many times how she had always wanted her breakfast in her room, but had never been able to have it, that I decided to give her that privilege in my house. I told Mary with some misgivings, and showed her the things I had bought. To my surprise, Mary assented joyfully. I never knew why until after Flora left. Then Mary told me. I even selected the china she was to use on the breakfast-tray. It was blue and gold. Flora loved blue. Then I took a final look at everything, gave a few last orders, and dismissed all worry from my mind.

Her room, *the guest chamber* of the Jardines, was fresh for her. No one had ever slept in that bed, fluttered those curtains, nor written at that desk. Flora would be its first occupant.

And how her blond beauty matched its pale blue and gold loveliness! It gave me thrills of delight to think of her in the midst of it all.

But of course it was Cary I loved. Flora simply fascinated me. She possessed the attractions of a Circe, but Cary was worth a million of her, and I knew it and I wanted her to have Artie Beg, or anybody else on earth she fancied. The whole proposition was as plain as day when I came to think about it. I was Cary's champion, Cary's friend, and intended Cary to win. Why, therefore, had I permitted myself to be inveigled into asking Flora to visit me, under the supposition that I was going to help her? It was not because Cary had begged me to. Not at all. It was Flora herself who had managed it, I reflected, and it gave me a bitter, uncomfortable twinge to realize that whatever Flora had wanted me to do, in our brief friendship, I had done, no matter whose judgment it went against.

Had the girl hypnotic power, or was I a weak fool to be flattered into doing her bidding?

I don't like to think of myself as a weak fool, even for the sake of argument.

The two girls had hated each other at sight, as was natural. Cary admitted the reason with glorious frankness.

"Of course I hate her," she said, with a lift of her sleek brown head, "didn't she usurp my prerogatives at the wedding? The best man belongs, for that evening alone, to the maid of honour—he can't escape it—it is his fate. Common civility should have chained him to my chariot wheels, but with that white-headed Lilith at work on him, with her half-shut eyes, she had him queered before he even saw me. But wait. My turn will come."

Flora said to me:

"Of course I hate her, because *you* love her. You love her better than you love me. You have known her longer—that's the only reason! She doesn't care *that* for you. It's because you are married, and can give her a good time that she pretends to care for you. *I* know. Oh, you may laugh and think I am jealous or insane or anything you like. Well, then, I *am* jealous, for I love you better than anybody in the world, and I want you to love me in the same way. I love you better than I love my mother—or my father—or even Artie Beg! And I am jealous of every one you speak to. I am jealous most of all of Aubrey, for you have eyes for no one on earth but him. I could hate him when I think of it."

At that I *did* laugh, but she was a good actress, and said it as if she meant it.

Flora always acted as if she knew of my repressed childhood, and of how, all my life, I had thirsted for praise. No matter if it had been put on with a trowel, as hers undoubtedly was, I would have wrapped myself in its tropical warmth and luxuriance, and never paused to quarrel with its effulgence. While dear old Cary let her actions speak, and seldom put her affection for me into words. But she had been on the eve of sailing for a winter in Egypt when my hurried wedding preparations and frantic telegram arrested her. The party sailed without her, and she did not try to follow. And that was only one of the many sacrifices she had made for me, and made without a word, too.

She was a girl of thought and of ideas, but unfortunately she was a great heiress, and fortune-hunters had made her suspicious and cynical. Only Aubrey and I knew how glorious she could be when she let herself out and expressed her real self.

The first thing Flora did to make me uncomfortable was to pump the Angel about Artie's law-suit.

It was so intricate, so long drawn out, and so enormous in its proportions, that it bade fair to resemble the famous Jarndyce and Jarndyce. We had never mentioned it to Artie, but Flora, after a few reluctant words from Aubrey, persuaded Artie, in the easiest way imaginable, to tell her everything about it, from its inception. She told me she had even read half a dozen of her uncle's law-books, which bore upon the knotty points Artie had described to her. Instead of arousing his suspicions of mercenary motives, her innocent manner and flowerlike face deceived him into believing that her interest was very commendable. She explained that she had always wanted to study law, but that her father wouldn't let her, so that she always coaxed her friends to describe their law-suits to her, and then she read up on them by herself. Artie thought this was wonderful. So it was.

Cary would never listen to a word about it, nor read about it in the papers; nor could she be inveigled into expressing an opinion about it one way or the other. Her pride revolted from appearing even to know that he had such prospects, faint and distant though they were.

When Flora came, Mary put on her spectacles before she opened the door. I noticed the look she gave all three of us. It did not speak well for Flora.

But, at first, her shyness and modesty left nothing to be desired. Her clothes were simple even to plainness, her voice soft and deprecating, and her manner deferential in the extreme. She was always asking advice, and where that advice was given, she always followed it. Flattery could go no further.

Artie came to see her, morning, noon, and night. I was horrified to discover how far things seemed to have progressed, for, after all, it was Cary who *must* have Artie if she wanted him.

Cary called on Flora once, and we returned it, but she did not come again. So I resolved on a dinner, and Cary promised to come. The others were to be the Jimmies, Bee, and three more persons so insignificant, so vapid, so entirely not worth describing that, in a race, they would not even be mentioned as "also rans." In short, they were the typical dinner-guests the hostess always fills in with.

I worked hard on that dinner. Flora offered to help, but Mary, without actually refusing her assistance, managed to do without it, and I did not realize until afterward how quickly Flora accepted her fate, and curled herself up luxuriously on Aubrey's couch in Aubrey's particular corner to read, while I bleached the almonds which she had offered to do.

Flora kept me well informed of the progress of Artie's passion for her, and I could do nothing. I was surprised at her confiding such details to any one, dismayed for Cary's sake, and worried as to how it would turn out.

Finally the evening of the dinner came. I dressed and ran out to the kitchen to see if everything was all right, for Mary was so jealous she refused to let me engage an assistant, but doggedly persisted in preparing and serving the dinner entirely by herself.

To my surprise, I found the dining-room and kitchen shades pulled up to the tops of the windows, while every handsome dish Mary intended to use, and all the extra silver, were carefully placed on top of the laundry-tubs. Mary, apparently unconscious of observation, was flying around with pink cheeks, and the eyes behind the spectacles snapping with excitement.

"Don't say a word, Missus," she said, sitting on her heels before the oven door. "I did it for the benefit of the rubber factory opposite. They think I don't notice, but look at them windows. Not a light in any of 'em, but all the curtains moving just a little. Do they think I don't know there's a rubber behind every damn one of 'em? Don't laugh, Missus dear, and don't look over there, whatever you do. If they want a look at the things we eat, why let 'em! They know what they cost, but I'll bet they never do more than ask the price of 'em, and then buy soup-bones and canned vegetables for their own stomachs."

Mary didn't say stomachs, but much of Mary's conversation does not look well in print.

"And just wait till I take in the 'peche flambee'!" she chuckled. "I'll bet they'll order out the fire department!"

I said nothing, for the very excellent reason that there was really nothing to say. Mary has a way of being rather conclusive. There was no use in remonstrating or telling her not to, for she simply would not have obeyed me, so I forbore to give the order.

Flora heard Mary let Artie Beg in, and ran down the corridor to meet him. She was a vision in white—her graduation dress—with her snowy shoulders rising modestly from a tulle bertha. I paused in order to let her greet him first, and, to my consternation, before I could make known my presence, I heard her say, plaintively:

"Aren't you going to kiss me?"

Then with a stifled groan Artie flung his arms around her, pressing her to him as if he would never let her go. Then he pushed her away from him almost roughly, and Flora laughed a low, tantalizing laugh, and crept back to him to lean her head on his shoulder, and lay her arms around his neck.

I turned and fled. I fairly stampeded down the hall, running full tilt against Aubrey, and nearly folding him up.

"Oh! Oh!" I gasped, dancing up and down before him excitedly.

He seized both my hands.

"Hold still, Faith! What's the matter? Tell me!"

"They're engaged!" I wailed. "I'm too late! Cary has lost him!"

"Who?"

"Artie and Flora."

"What makes you think so?"

"He's kissing her! And she asked him to, just as if she had a

Lilian Bell

right. I would not think so much of it, if he had just grabbed her and kissed her without a word, for she looks too witching, and any man might lose his head, but for her to ask for it—oh, what shall I do!"

"Hold on! You say she asked him to—tell me just how."

I told him.

The Angel put both hands in his pockets and whistled.

"Don't worry," he said. "They're not engaged."

I felt relieved at once, for the Angel does not write books from guesswork. He *knows* things.

But I was greatly confused at going back. Of course they did not know that I had seen and heard, and equally, of course, I could not tell them. But I had my confusion all to myself. Artie seemed about as usual (which he wouldn't have done if he had known that there was powder on his coat), and Flora was as cool as an iceberg.

It seems to me, as I look back, that that was the first time I suspected anything. It was almost uncanny to see her sitting there looking so shy and demure, when two minutes before she had begged a man to kiss her, and laughed that cool, tantalizing laugh, as of one who knew her power and revelled in the sight of her victim's struggles to escape.

I turned to Cary, my well-bred girl, my friend, with a feeling of relief, as if I had found a refuge. Cary flushed a little as she greeted Artie, and Flora's lip curled perceptibly.

I glanced at the Angel, and saw that he, too, had noticed it. But then, Aubrey sees everything. That is why he writes as he does. His manner as he greeted Cary was so cordial that it caused Artie to look up, and then, to my surprise, Artie got up from his chair, and came and stood by Cary and took her fan.

I wish you could have seen Flora's blue eyes turn green.

Then Bee and the Jimmies came, and, as usual, I straightway forgot everything else, and bent my energies toward playing the part of hostess so that Bee would not feel disgraced.

I followed her eye as it travelled over our gowns and around the apartment. Bee does not realize that she has silently appointed herself Superior General to the universe, so she was somewhat disconcerted, when, as she finally leaned back with a sigh which seemed to say, "This is really as well as anybody could do who didn't have me to consult with," to hear Aubrey say, slyly:

"Well, Bee, does it suit?"

Bee assumed her most Park Lane air, and replied:

"I don't know what you mean, Aubrey."

Then to avoid further pleasantries, Mary standing in the doorway, I marshalled them all out to the table.

Flora was between Aubrey and Artie, but I put Cary on the other side of Artie, while I took Jimmie by me, and mercilessly handed Mrs. Jimmie over to the "also rans."

Flora, who pretended jealousy of the Angel to veil her instinctive dislike of one who read her through and through, frankly turned her back on him, and tried all her wiles on Artie, which would not have disconcerted him, had not the

Also Ran commenced to smile and attract Mrs. Jimmie's attention to it.

This brought Artie from his trance sufficiently to cause him to turn his attention to Cary, but it was so palpably forced that Cary devoted herself with ardour to Jimmie, and left Artie speechless.

Then something spurred Flora to do a foolish thing. She deliberately began to bait Cary—to say things to annoy her—to try to mortify her. At first Cary refused to see what was evident to the rest of us. (Oh, my dinner-party was proving such a success!)

At this critical juncture, Mary appeared bearing the chafing-dish full of blazing, flaming peaches, and in watching me ladle the fiery liquid, hostilities were for the moment discontinued. Involuntarily, as Mary's satisfied countenance betokened her complete happiness at the successful culmination of the dinner, my eyes wandered to the dining-room windows. I had drawn the shades with my own hand, but some mysterious agent had been at work, for they were let fly to the very window-tops.

I glanced at Mary. She pressed her lips together with a whimsical twist, and surreptitiously raised a finger in sly warning.

"Them rubbers are having a fit!" she murmured in my ear, as she deferentially took a blazing peach from me, and placed it before Flora with a look so black it seemed to say:

"If you get your deserts, you little blister, it would set fire to you!"

They were talking about love when I began listening

again,—and Cary made some remark inaudible to me, which gave Flora the opportunity to say:

"Is it true, then, what I have heard? Were you ever disappointed in love?"

"Always!" said Cary, evenly.

Jimmie grinned and jogged my elbow.

"Isn't she a dandy?" he whispered. "Never turned a hair."

Flora flushed angrily because Artie laughed and looked appreciatively at Cary, as if really seeing her for the first time.

Every woman knows when that supreme moment comes—at least, every woman has who has liked a man before he has liked her. She feels it without looking at him. She knows it from the innermost consciousness of her being. "He is looking at me," says her heart, "for the first time, with the eyes which a man has for a woman."

Many a man has been selected first, as Cary selected Artie, and been wooed by her as modestly and legitimately as she did, without suspecting that he did not take the initiative every time.

So a little modest courage and restrained self-reliance crept into Cary's manner, which had never been there before, and I, believing implicitly in the Angel's *ipse dixit* that Flora and the best man were not engaged, had visions of the first bridesmaid's winning her lost place with, and, oh, making him pay for his neglect.

If man only knew how heavily a flouted woman, after she

has safely won him, does make him pay for his bad taste, he would be more careful.

But Artie never knew. He sat there, listening to the biting words which passed back and forth between Flora and Cary, without his modesty permitting him to realize that he was the stake these two clever girls were throwing mental dice for.

But Jimmie knew, for his blue eyes turned black, and his cigarettes burned out in two puffs, and his nervous hands clenched and unclenched in his wicked wish to say something to aggravate the affair. Finally, meeting my derisive grin, he wrenched my little finger under the table, under pretence of picking up my handkerchief, and whispered:

"Oh, Lord, give me strength to keep out of this row!"

I laughed, of course, and so missed something, for the next thing I heard, the conversation had become more personal, and Flora was saying:

"Love is an acquisition. The more you have, the more you want."

"Pardon me," said Cary. "To my mind, love is a sacrifice. Yet the more you give, the more you gain."

"But I don't want to believe that!" pouted Flora, charmingly. "That is a cruel, ascetic conception of love. It makes me shiver, like reading the New Testament."

For the first time Artie spoke.

"You prefer, then, the Song of Solomon?" And the Angel brought his hand down on the table a little heavily, and looked at me.

"Yes, I do!" laughed Flora, thinking she had scored. "And I know—because I have loved!"

"You have loved, have you?" said Cary, leaning forward to look at her across Artie's tucked shirt-front. "Then if you have, truly and deeply, as a woman can, when she meets the man who is her mate, can you jest so lightly about love being an acquisition? Are you thinking of his income and what he can give you more than your father has been able to do? Does your idea of marriage consist of dinner-parties and routs? Or do you think of the man himself? Of his noble qualities of heart and mind? Does not the idea of permanent prosperity sometimes fade, and in its place do you not sometimes see the man you love, poor, neglected by his friends, and jeered by his enemies? Does he not sometimes appear to you stretched on a weary bed of sickness? Can you picture yourself his only friend, his only helper, his only comforter? If he were crippled for life, would you go out to try to earn bread for two, rejoicing that Fate had only taken his strength to toil, and not his strength to love? Would you still count yourself a blessed woman if you knew that everything were swept away but the love of a man worth loving like that?"

Flora quailed, and drew back, abashed and a little frightened, but Artie's face was a study. At a sign from Aubrey, I looked at Mrs. Jimmie and rose. Just behind me, as I turned, I heard Artie whisper to Cary:

"Tell me, have *you* ever loved like that?"

And Cary's murmured reply:

"Not yet, but—I could."

After that, Flora's fascination seemed to wane. Mrs. Jimmie

never had liked her, and as we went into the drawing-room she gave Cary one of her rare and highly prized caresses, which Cary received gratefully.

As for Artie, he never left Cary's side. He was the first to follow us to the drawing-room, for as I always let men smoke at the table, we always leave it *en masse.*

He said little, but he listened to every word Cary spoke, and he watched her as if fascinated.

I was jubilant, and my sober old Angel almost permitted himself to look pleased, but not quite. The Angel is never reckless with his emotions.

Dinner had been over about two hours, and Mrs. Jimmie was beginning to look at the clock, when Aubrey approached and whispered:

"I haven't heard a sound in the kitchen since dinner, and Mary hasn't entered the dining-room. Don't you think we would better take a look at her?"

The kitchen was separated from the dining-room by only the butler's pantry. As we opened the swinging door, a figure holding a chafing-dish in both hands attempted to rise from the cracker-box, but sank back again, shaking with laughter.

"It's me, Boss dear! Don't look so scared, but I'm drunk as a fool. How many of them awful peaches did you eat, Missis?"

"Only one," I said.

"And you, Boss?"

"Only one. How many did you eat?"

"Only half a one, but I finished all the juice in the dish—"

"Juice!" I cried. "Why, Mary, that was brandy and kirschwasser, and two or three other things."

"Don't I know it? But I never thought, Missis dear, I came here to rubber at that fight between Miss Farquhar and the little blister—"

"Mary!"

"Not a word more, Missis dear, if you don't like it! But anyhow I came here to—rest myself, and I began absent-mindedly to take a sip out of this big spoon here, and soon it was all gone. Then when you all went into the other room, I tried to get up, but my legs didn't want to, and, be the powers, they haven't wanted to since, though I've tried 'em every two minutes or so. I've just set here, helpless as a new-born babe that can't roll over in its crib. I meant to flag the first one of you that went past the door, for if somebody would prop me up in front of the sink, I could begin on a pile of dishes there big enough to scare a dog from his cats."

Aubrey and I leaned against each other in silent but hysterical delight. Mary was deeply pleased to see us so diverted.

Her legs recovered sufficiently before we left for her to walk to the sink, while we went back to our guests.

Every one was leaving, and Artie was taking Cary home. I looked to see how Flora took it, but her appealing blue eyes were fixed in their most appealing way upon the Also Ran, who was plainly undergoing thrills of exquisite torture therefrom. Jimmie gave one look at the tableau, and turned toward the door with his tongue in his cheek.

After that curious evening, there seemed to be a tremendous emotional upheaval. Artie hardly came near Flora, and when he did call, appeared to derive much satisfaction from gazing at her with a quizzical look in his eyes which seemed to annoy her excessively. The Also Ran was omnipresent, and was instant in season, out of season. But instead of arousing Artie's jealousy, this seemed only to amuse him.

Finally the cause of Artie's visits developed. He blurted it out to me one day with the red face of a shamed schoolboy.

"Faith, I wish you'd do me the favour to ask Cary Farquhar here some evening, and let me know! I've been going there till I'm ashamed to face the butler, but I never can see her alone, and the last two times she has sent down her excuses, and wouldn't see me at all."

I could have squealed for joy, but, mindful of Cary's dignity, I said:

"I don't believe she'd come, Artie. I'm afraid—"

"Afraid that she'd suspect that I would be here too? I don't believe I've made it as plain as that!" he interrupted.

"Do you mean to say that you are really and truly—?"

"I mean just that," he said, with a new earnestness in his manner, that I never had noted before.

"Oh, Artie!" I cried. "I'm *so* glad! But what if she's—"

"Don't say it! It makes me cold all over to think of it. That's why I want you to ask her here. I've *got* to see her. Why, Faith, she's—really, Faith, she's the *only* girl in the world, now *isn't* she?"

"So I've thought for years!" I cried, warmly.

"Talk about love being instantaneous," said Artie, plunging his hands into his pockets, and striding up and down. "I've loved her and loved her *hard* ever since she explained what love meant to her that night at your dinner. Why, if I could get her to love *me* that way, I'd be richer than John D! But shucks! She never will! What am *I*, I'd like to know, to expect such a miracle?"

"You're very nice!" I stuttered, in my haste, "and just the man for her, both Aubrey and I think, but I'll tell you where the trouble is. She thinks you belong to Flora."

"Never!" replied Artie, vehemently. "I never *thought* of marrying Flora. She—well, she sort of appealed to me—you know how! She wanted me to help her to understand golf. She said it made her feel so out of it not to know what people were talking about who played the game—you know she was a poke at college, and didn't go in for athletics at all. Well, you can understand it when you look at her. *She* couldn't get into a sweater and a short skirt and play basket-ball, now could she? She'd be wanting some man always about to hold her things or pitch the ball for her. She is such a dependent little thing. Then she had always wanted to study law and her people wouldn't let her—don't blame 'em for it!—but she wanted me to help her to understand it just for practice, she said, so I tried to. But as to *marrying* her! Well, to tell the truth—she—er—she does things—I mean, I think her emotions are a little too volcanic to suit *me,* and I'm no prude.

"You'll tell Cary this, won't you, Faith? All but that last. Explain how I came to get tangled up with the girl. You can do it so she won't suspect that you're working for me. You can bring it in casually, without bungling it. Tell her I never gave a serious thought to Flora in my life."

"I will, and I'll get her here for you!" I cried, as he rose to go.

I followed him to the door, and as I closed it after him the door of the butler's pantry opened noiselessly, and there stood old Mary with her finger on her lip. She motioned me to precede her, and she followed me down the hall to my room and into it, carefully closing the door behind her. "Missis," she whispered, kneeling down beside my chair. "Scold me! Do! I've been made the real fool of by that little blister. Lord, if I wouldn't like to take her across my knee with a fat pine shingle in my good right hand. Listen! She heard you at the telephone, and knew you expected Mr. Beguelin this afternoon, so she comes to me just after lunch and she says to me, 'Mary, Mr. Beguelin is coming this evening, so I think I'll take a little nap on the couch if you'll cover me up with the brown rug.' The brown rug, see? Just the colour of the couch, and the one I always keep put away for the Boss. Of course I couldn't refuse after she said you said to give it to her—"

"I didn't," I interrupted.

"I know it. I know it now! But the little devil knew that I was going out, and that you would answer the door yourself—"

"Mary!" I shrieked, in a whisper. "She wasn't in there all the time, was she?"

"That's just what she was! Listening to every word you said. I just came in a minute ago, or I'd have let you know. But he got up to go, just as I had my hand on the door-knob."

"What shall I do?" I murmured, distractedly. Then, after a pause, I said, "Perhaps she was asleep and didn't hear!"

Mary gave me such a contemptuous look that I hurriedly apologized.

Then the Angel came in, and I told Mary to go, and then I told him everything. He thought quite awhile before speaking.

"Do you care for her very much, Faith dear?" he said, in his dear, gentle way.

"If she has done the abominable thing that Mary says, I'll— hate her! I'll turn her out of the house!" I cried, viciously.

"Ah!" said Aubrey, in a satisfied tone. He knows I wouldn't, but it does do me so much good to threaten to do the awful things I'd like to do if I were a cruel woman.

He rose and left the room. I started to follow him, but he waved me back.

"I won't be gone a moment. Wait for me here."

I waited three or four years, and then, when I had grown white-haired with age, he came back.

"Begin at the beginning, tell everything, and don't skip a word," I demanded.

"Well," he began, obediently. "She was sobbing gently—not for effect this time. I went in softly, and asked her what the matter was. She said she had been out all the afternoon to see a friend who had just been obliged to place her mother in a lunatic asylum, and she was crying for sympathy. Then, as she saw me look at my rug, she said Mary had left the rug out for her to take a nap early in the afternoon, and that she had intended to, but had decided to go out instead. Now what

I object to is the style of her lying. I admire a good lie, but a clumsy, misshapen, rippled affair like that one is an abomination in the sight of the Lord."

I stood up with a flaming face.

"Don't get excited," said Aubrey. "She is going home to-morrow. Keep calm to-night, and the next time you see Artie, he will relieve all your feelings by what he will say."

"Why? What does he know?"

"Well, the Also Ran admires athletic girls, you know, not being able to sit astride a horse himself, and through his boasting Artie has discovered that Flora is a crack golf player—won the cup for her college in her junior year."

I fell on the bed in a fit of hysterical laughter.

"If that's the way you are going to take it, I feel that I can tell you the worst," said Aubrey, with a relieved face. "The fact is, I believe that that girl has a game on with the Also Ran."

"Oh, *no*, Aubrey!" I cried. "I know that she is too desperately in love with Artie to care about anybody else. She is so fascinating I have but one fear, and that is that Artie will come under her sway again. If he does, Cary would never forgive it."

"You are barking up the wrong tree, my dear," said my husband. "It is far more likely that Artie has already gone too far with Flora for Cary to forgive, and that's why she won't see him."

At that, I tossed my head, for I felt that I knew how both Cary and Flora loved better than Aubrey did. Flattering myself, also, that I knew men pretty well, I had my doubts about the strength of Artie's character. It takes real courage for a man to be true to one woman, if another woman has pitted her fascinations against him.

I intended to avoid Flora, but I found her lying in wait for me, and beckoning me from the doorway. I went in, and at once, in order to seem natural, remarked upon her red eyes. But it seems that that was exactly what she wanted me to do. The girl had no pride. She *wanted* me to pity her.

"I'm ready to kill myself!" she cried. "I am perfectly sure that Artie has only been flirting with me and that some one has come between us. You can't want Cary to have him, or why did you invite me here, and arrange for me to see so much of him, and try so hard to bring us together? You are not two-faced like that, I hope?"

I was too bewildered to speak. Yet how could I answer her questions? Before I left her, I was convinced that it was all my fault. I told Aubrey so.

"Nonsense!" he said, quite roughly for him. "I think Mary's name for Flora is a good one. She is a little blister."

"No," I said, "she is not bad at heart. She is simply an impulsive, uncontrolled little animal, and more frank in her loves than most of us. That's all."

I saw the Angel set his lips together as if he could say something if he only dared, but his way of managing me is to give me my head and let circumstances teach me. He never forces Nature's hand.

Flora's visit was to have terminated the next day, but, to Aubrey's intense disgust and my utter rout, she begged for just three days more, and before I knew it I had consented. As I hurriedly left the room after consenting, I turned suddenly and met her gaze. Her eyes were a mere slit in her face, so narrowed and crafty they were. And the look she shot at me was a look of hatred.

Too bewildered by this curious girl's inexplicable actions to try to unravel my emotions and come to a decision regarding her, I kept out of her way all I could. I was simply waiting— waiting impatiently for the three days to pass. I only hoped that Artie would not come again while she was here.

But, alas, the very next morning I was at the telephone when I heard Flora run to the door to let somebody in, and before I could speak I heard her say, in that surprised, complaining tone of hers, "Aren't you going to kiss me?" and then—well, I got up and slammed the door so hard that the key fell out.

What a fool Artie was? What fools *all* men were, not to be able to keep faith with a woman, and such a woman as Cary Farquhar! I rushed from the study into my room, and burst into a storm of tears, in the midst of which Aubrey found me.

"Poor little Faith! Poor, discouraged, little match-maker!" he said, smoothing my hair. But at that last I sat up and shook his hand off.

"It's so *disgusting* of him!" I stammered. "If you could have heard him when he was talking about Flora!"

"How do you know it was Artie who came in?" said Aubrey, gently.

I opened my mouth and simply stared at him. Then I went to the glass, smoothed my hair and straightened my belt.

"Where are you going?" asked my husband.

"I am going to *see*!" I exclaimed. "And if it *isn't* Artie—if she is kissing every man that comes into this house, I'll—I'll *kill* her."

"What! You'll kill her if you find that Artie is not the faithless wretch you were crying about?"

"Oh, Aubrey! How *can* you?" I cried.

He tried to catch me as I flew past, but I eluded him, and started firmly down the long hall. But in spite of myself, my feet dragged. What was Flora attempting? Did she hate me as her look implied? Did she love Artie as she declared, or was she simply endeavouring to get married, and so save herself from a life of teaching, which she openly detested?

I kept on, however, goaded by my righteous indignation. To my astonishment I found, not Artie, but the Also Ran, with Flora frankly in his arms.

They sprang up at my swift entrance, and the man had the grace to look furiously confused. Flora never even changed colour. I asked no questions. I simply stood before them in accusing silence. But my look was black and ominous. Flora gave one swift glance at my uncompromising attitude, and then, with a modesty and grace and sweet appealing humility impossible to describe, she came a step toward me, holding out her arms and saying, plaintively:

"Won't you congratulate me? We are engaged."

I was struck dumb—that is, I would have been struck dumb, if I had not been rendered not only speechless, but unable to move by the actions of the man. Entirely unmindful of my presence, he sprang toward Flora, stammering, brokenly:

"Do you mean it, dear? Have you decided already? You said six months! You are sure you mean it?"

Then, not seeing the angry colour flame into Flora's pale, calm face, he turned to me, saying, brokenly:

"Oh, Mrs. Jardine! She has teased me so! I never dreamed she would decide so quickly. And I—you will forgive me! but I love her so!"

I looked away from his twitching face to Flora, and mentally resolved never to call him an Also Ran again. He did not deserve it. I am seldom sarcastic, but I knew Flora would understand.

"Flora," I said, distinctly, "you are to be congratulated."

Then I turned and left them.

The very day that Flora left, Cary came back to me.

"Well," she said, tentatively, "what do you think of her?"

"Well," I answered, cautiously, "I don't know."

Cary looked at me in disgust.

"Your loyalty amounts to nothing short of blindness and stupidity," she remarked, severely. "As for me, I am going to look at the nest the viper has left."

So saying, she got up and went into the blue room, Aubrey and I meekly following.

Pinned to the pillow was a note directed to me. Cary unpinned and handed it to me.

"Cleverest and best of women," it began, "Many thanks for your delightful hospitality. I have enjoyed it to the full—far more, indeed, than you know. Look under the mattress of this bed and you will understand."

We tore the bed to pieces without speaking. Then Aubrey and Cary looked at each other and laughed.

"*Now* will you believe," said Cary.

There were cigarette-boxes full of nothing but butts and ashes. There were three of my low-cut bodices. There were some of Aubrey's ties and a number of my best handkerchiefs.

I said nothing. I simply stared.

"We all knew of these things, Faith dear," said Aubrey, "but even if you had caught her wearing your clothes or smoking, we knew she would lie out of it, so we waited."

"We knew she hated you so that she couldn't help telling you," added Cary.

"Hated me?" I murmured. "What for?"

Cary blushed furiously, and looked at Aubrey.

"Has Ar—Have you—" I stammered, eagerly.

Cary nodded and Aubrey looked wise. Then Cary and I rushed for each other.

While we still had our arms around each other crying for joy, Mary appeared at the door with her apron filled with the neat little jars of jellies and marmalades I had got for Flora's breakfasts. They had not been opened. Mary regarded me with grim but whimsical defiance.

"The little blister never got a blamed one of 'em, Missis!" she said.

# CHAPTER VII

## THE PRICE OF QUIET

Mr. and Mrs. Jimmie were among our frequent visitors in the new apartment. Jimmie can never realize that I am really married, and in view of our manifold travelling experiences together he regards the Angel with an eye in which sympathy and apprehension are mingled.

His congratulations at the wedding were unique. "I'd like to congratulate you, old man," he said, wringing the Angel's hand, "but honestly I think you are up against it."

To me at their first call he said:

"What will you do with such a man—you, who have gone scrapping through life, browbeating gentle souls like myself into giving you your own way on every point, and letting you ride rough-shod over us without a protest? *He* requires consideration and tact and a degree of courtesy—none of which you possess. And you can't drag him away from his writing to go to the morgue or a pawn-shop with you the way you did me in Europe. And most of all he must have quiet. Gee whiz! There will be hours together when you must hold your tongue. You'll die!"

"No, I won't," I declared. "You don't know him. He is an Angel." And with that the argument closed, for Jimmie went off into such a fit of laughter that he choked, and his wife came in a fright to find me pounding him on the back with unnecessary force.

"But why," said Jimmie, when order had been restored, "did you take an apartment, when Aubrey's chief requirement is absence of noise! Furthermore, why do you live in New York, that city which reigns supreme in its accumulation of unnecessary bedlam?"

"Ah, we have thought of all those things," I said, proudly. "First, we avoided a street paved with cobblestones. Second, we took the top floor. Third, there are no houses opposite— only the Park."

"But best of all," said the Angel, speaking for the first time, as Jimmie noted, "it is in the lease that no children are allowed, for children, after all, are the most noise-producing animals which exist. So if an apartment can be noise-proof—"

"Exactly," cut in Jimmie. "If!"

"That's what I say—if it can," said the Angel, "this one should prove so. Faith and I certainly took sufficient pains in selecting it."

"Well, I don't want to discourage you," said Jimmie, and then, after the manner of those who begin their sentences in that way, he proceeded to discourage us in every sort of ingenious fashion which lay at his command. Verily, friends are invaluable in domestic crises!

Nevertheless, his gloomy prophecies disturbed us. We tried

to make light of our fears—to pooh-pooh them—to pretend a scorn for Jimmie's opinions, which in secret we were far from feeling, for the fact remained that the Jimmies were experienced and we were not. "Living in an apartment," Jimmie had declared, "is like driving. You may have perfect control over your own horse, but you have constantly to fear the bad driving of other people."

These words kept ringing in our ears. We never forgot for a moment that there were people under us. We crept in gently if a supper after the theatre kept us out until two in the morning. We never allowed the piano to be played after ten in the evening nor before breakfast. We gave up the loved society of our dog, and boarded him in the country because dogs, cats, and parrots were not allowed.

But day by day we found that each one of these self-inflicted maxims was being violated by all the other residents. Singing popular songs, a pianola, half a dozen fox terriers, laughing and shouting good nights in the corridors kept us awake half the night, and worst of all, what we patiently submitted to as visitors with children, we, to our horror, discovered were residents with children, and children of the most detested sort at that. Five of these hyenas in human form lived below us. Their parents were of the easy-going sort. They had all come from a plantation in Virginia, and they had brought their plantation manners with them.

Now, ordinary children are bad enough, and even well-trained ones at that, in the matter of noise, but the noises made by the Gottlieb children were something too appalling to be called by the plain, ordinary word. They had never learned to close a door. They slammed it, and every cup and saucer on our floor danced in reply. When their mother wanted them, she never thought of going to the room they were in to speak to them. She sat still and called. They yelled back defiant negatives or whining questions, and then the negro nurse was sent, and she hauled them in by one arm, their legs dragging rebelliously on the floor and their other arm clutching wildly at pillars or furniture to delay their reluctant progress.

They had a piano, and all five of them took piano lessons. Out of the kindness of their hearts they invited the three children who lived opposite them on the same floor to practise on their piano, so that from seven in the morning until nine at night we were treated to five-finger exercises and scales. Their favourite diversion was a game which consisted of the entire eight racing through their apartment, jumping the nursery bed, and landing against the wall beyond. They had hardwood floors and no rugs.

And the Angel must have quiet in which to write!

We discussed the situation, and resolved to take action. Move? Certainly not! We had done our best in taking this apartment, and we modestly felt that our best was not to be sneezed at. We would make the other people move,—the impertinent people who had dared to produce children off the premises, and then to introduce them ready-made in a non-children apartment-house. Of course a landlord could not protect himself against the home-grown article, so to speak, but he could defend both himself and us against articles of foreign manufacture, and so flagrantly, as evidenced by the names of these "made in Germany."

Other noises which stunned us were remediable by other means. For example, the janitor of the apartment-house which stood next had a pleasant little habit of three times a day emptying some dozen or more metal garbage-cans in the stone-paved court, and as these with their lids and handles merrily jingled back into place, a roar as if from a boiler factory rose, reverberating between the high buildings until, when it reached the sensitive ears of the Jardines, it created pandemonium.

At such times the Angel used to look at me in dumb but helpless misery. I tried bribing the janitor, but they changed so often I couldn't afford it. Then, without a word to the Angel, I appealed to the Health Department. I made a stirring plea. I set forth that not only our health, but our lives (by which I meant our pocketbooks, because the Angel could not write in a noise), were threatened, and I implored protection.

An Irishman answered. God bless soft-hearted, pleasant-spoken Irishmen! This one rescued us from a slow death by torture. He was amenable to blarney. He got it. The result was that never again did any of the serial of janitors, which ran continuously next door, empty garbage-cans in the court.

Rendered jubilant by this victory, we confidently prepared to meet the agents of our building. But before we could arrange this, Considine, the novelist who had come to New York for the winter, called. He was one of the Angel's dearest friends, and we greeted him with effusion.

"I've come to say good-bye," he said at once. "I'm off to-morrow for my farm."

"For a visit?" I cried, unwilling to believe the worst.

"No, for good. I'm done. I'm finished. New York has put an end to me!"

"Why, how do you mean?" we asked, in a breath.

"The noise! The blankety, blankety, et cetera noise of this ditto ditto town! The remainder of these remarks will be sent in a plain, sealed envelope upon application and the receipt of a two-cent stamp!"

The Angel and I looked at each other. We dared not speak.

"How—why—" I faltered at last.

It was all Considine needed—perhaps more than he needed —to set him going.

"I came here under contract, as you know. I was behindhand in my work, but I hoped that the inspiration I would receive from the society of my fellow authors would give me an impetus I lacked in the country. There I often have to spur myself to my work. Here I hoped to work more steadily and with less effort. Ye gods!" He got up and strode around the apartment. "Ye gods! What fallacies we provincials believe! I was in heaven on my farm and didn't know it! And from that celestial paradise of peace and quiet and tranquillity of nature, I deliberately came to this—with a view of bettering my surroundings! When I think of it—when I consider the money I have spent and the time I have lost—" he stopped by reason of choking.

"Why, do you know," he began again, squaring around on the Angel, "I've spent twenty thousand dollars on that apartment of mine, trying to make it sound-proof so that I could make ten thousand by writing! I rented the apartment below me—had to, in order to get a fellow out whose son was learning the violin. I've bribed, threatened, enjoined, and at the last a subway explosion of dynamite broke all the double windows and mirrors, knocked down my Italian chandeliers, and—people tell me I have no redress! Now they have started some kind of a drilling machine in the next block that runs all night, and I can't sleep. New York to live in? New York to work in? Why, I'd rather be a yellow dog in

Louisville than to be Mayor of New York!"

But before he could go the bell rang and Mr. and Mrs. Jimmie walked in, so then Considine came back for ten minutes, and stayed two hours.

We told them what we had been discussing, and then we all took comfortable chairs. Cigars and tall glasses with ice and decanters and things that fizz were produced, and, as Jimmie said, "we had such a hammerfest on the City of New York as the old town hadn't experienced in many a long day."

But then, when you come to think of it, didn't she deserve it?

In New York the elevated trains thundering over your head and darkening the street, surface electric cars beneath them being run at lightning speed, the street paved with cobblestones over which delivery carts are being driven at a pace which is cruelty to animals, form a combination of noises compared to which a battery of artillery in action is a lullaby, and which I defy any other city in the world to equal. A hen crossing a country lane in front of a carriage, squawking and wild-eyed, is a picture of my state of mind whenever I have a street to cross. Yesterday there were two street-car accidents and one runaway, which I saw with my own eyes in an hour's outing, and I had no sooner locked myself in my sixth-floor apartment with a sigh of relief at being saved from sudden death when a crash came in the street below, and by hanging out of the window I saw that an electric car had struck a plate-glass delivery wagon in the rear, upset it, smashed the glass, thrown the horse on his side, and so pushed them, horse, cart, and all, for a quarter of a block before the car could be stopped. I shrieked loud and long, but in the noise of the city no one heard me, and all the good it did was to ease my own mind.

New York is a good place to come to, to be amused, or to spend money, but as a city of terrific and unnecessary noises, there is not one in the world which can compare to it.

Scissors-grinders are allowed to use a bugle—a bugle, mind you, well known to be the most far-reaching sound of all sounds, and intended to carry over the roar of even artillery, else why is it used in a battle? So this bugling begins about seven in the morning, and penetrates the most hermetically sealed apartments. Then the street-cleaners, the "White Wings," garbage and ash-can men begin their deadly rounds, and the clang of dashing empty metal cans on the stone-paved courts and areas reverberates between high buildings until one longs for the silence of the grave.

The noise and shock of blasting rock is incessant. They are blasting all along the Hudson shore and in Central Park. It sounds like cannonading, and the succession of explosions sometimes wakens one before dawn or after midnight with the frightened conviction that a foreign fleet is upon us to force us to reduce the tariff. The blasting occasionally goes a little too far, and breaks windows or brings down pieces of the ceiling. Last week it caved in a house and broke some arms and legs of the occupants. One woman went into convulsions, and was rigid for hours from the shock, but as nobody was killed no action was taken.

Old clothes men are permitted a string of bells on their carts, which all jangle out of tune and at once, while street-cries of all descriptions abound in such numbers and of such a quality that I often wonder that the very babies trundled by in their perambulators do not go into spasms with the confusion of it.

Considine and I stated all this with some excusable heat while the Angel was serving our guests with what their different tastes demanded. It always gives me a feeling of unholy joy seeing Mrs. Jimmie trying to join her husband in his low pleasures. She regarded it as a religious duty to take beer when he did while we were abroad, but in England and here he takes whiskey and soda, so as champagne is not always on tap in people's houses, sometimes she tries to emulate his example.

Have you ever seen anybody take cod-liver oil? Well, that is the look which comes over Mrs. Jimmie's face when the odour of whiskey assails her aristocratic nostrils. Nevertheless she valiantly sits the whole evening through with her long glass in her hand. The ice melts and the whole mess grows warm and nauseous, but she hangs on, sipping at it with an air of determined enjoyment painful to see. If she did as she would like, she would either hold her nose and gulp it all down at once or else she would fling glass and all out of the window.

In vain we all try to make it easy for her to refuse. If we don't offer it she looks hurt, so the kindest thing we can do is to pretend we notice nothing, and to let her believe that she is her husband's boon companion, since that is her futile ambition.

Jimmie crossed his feet, blew a cloud of smoke into the air, and carried on the attack by saying:

"London, Paris, and Berlin all put together cannot furnish the noise of New York, while the roar of Chicago is the stillness of a cathedral compared to it. And most of it, I may be allowed to state, is entirely unnecessary. The papers are full of accounts of nervous collapses, the sanatoria are crowded, while I never heard as much about insanity in the whole of my life elsewhere as I have heard in New York in one year. There is not a day in which the papers do not contain some mention of insane wards in the city hospitals, but people here are so accustomed to it, that no one except a newcomer like yourself would be likely to notice it."

Considine nodded.

"I lay fully one-half of it to the incessant noises which prey upon even strong nerves for nine months of the year without our realizing them," he said, "and these so work upon the nervous system that it only takes a slight shock to bring about a collapse, and then no weeks in the country, no physic, no tonics can avail. It means a rest cure or the insane ward. It is typical of our American civilization. New Yorkers are the most nervous people I ever saw. The children are nervous; little street urchins, who should not know what nerves are, tremble with nervous tension, while the exodus to the country on Friday nights fairly empties the town. Everybody wants to 'get away from the noise,' and it is an undisputed fact that men who have no right to allow themselves the luxury take every Saturday as a holiday, so that in many lines of business so many men are known to be out of town on Saturdays that business is practically suspended on that day except for routine work. This is true to such an extent in no other city that I know of, and why? It is the noise. Distracted nature clamours for a cessation of it, and the unfortunate who cannot afford the luxury must pay the penalty. It is a question for the Board of Health."

"Poor old chap!" said Jimmie. "It comes hard enough on us common people, but how writing chaps like you and Aubrey stand it, I can't see. I should think you'd find New York the very devil to write in."

"In some ways we do," said the Angel, "but it has its compensations. For example, not even Paris is so beautifully situated as New York. The tall office buildings in the lower end of town look down upon river sights and shipping with a broad expanse of blue water and green shores which a man would cross the ocean to see on the other side. The Hudson beautifies the West Side. Central Park is in my eyes the most beautiful park I ever saw. With its rocks and rolling greens, its trees and wild flowers, it forms a spot of loveliness that makes in the midst of the hot, rushing, busy city a dream of soothing repose. Washington Heights is a crowning wilderness looking down upon the city from Fort George, while the Sound and a glimpse of the village beyond seen through the faint blue haze of distance lend a touch of fairylike enchantment. The Jersey shore and the Palisades are one long drawn out joy, so that, turn where you will, you find New York beautiful."

"Then, too," said Mrs. Jimmie, speaking for the first time, "New York is old, and say what you will you feel the charm of the established, and it gives you a sense of satisfaction to realize that you can't detect the odour of varnish and new paint. New York has got beyond it, and has begun to take on the gray of age."

"The churches show this," I cut in. "They are beautiful stepping-places in the rush of city life. They cool and steady, and their history and traditions form a restful contrast to the bustle of the marketplace."

"But as to those who worship in these beautiful spots," said Considine, "it is safe to say that church parade in Fifth Avenue is an even smarter spectacle than church parade in Hyde Park, for American women have an air, a carriage, and a taste in dress which English women as a race can never acquire. In Hyde Park on Sunday morning, during the season, one will see half a dozen beauties whose clothes are Parisian and the loveliness of whose whole effect almost takes the breath away, but the general run of the other

Lilian Bell

women makes one want to close one's eyes. In America the average woman is lovely enough to make each one worth looking at, while the word 'frump,' which is continually useful in England, might almost be dropped from the American language.

"As to manners in New York," he went on, "well, patriotic as I am, American manners in public in any city almost make me long for the outward politeness and inward insincerity of the Gallic nations. Russians and Poles are the only ones I have observed to be alike both in public and in private. In New York street-car etiquette or the etiquette of any public conveyance is something highly interesting from its variety of selfishness and rudeness."

"That is true," I said, "New York manners are seldom aggressively rude, except on the elevated trains. In other cities you are pushed about, walked over, elbowed aside, and often bodily hurt in crowds of their own selfish making. Not so in New York. Civilization has gone a step further here. In surface cars men never step on you, but they gently step ahead of you and take the seat you are aiming for, and if they can sit sidewise and occupy one and a half seats, and if you beg two of them to move closer together and let you have the remaining space, the two men may rise, one nearly always does and takes off his hat and begs you to have his place. Then all the eyes in the car are fixed on you—not reprovingly, or smilingly, or in derision or reproach, but earnestly, as if you form a social study which it might be worth their while to investigate. Never once during a year's observance of surface-car phenomena have I seen a row of luxuriously seated people make a movement to give place to a new-comer, no matter how old or how well gowned she may be. Even ladies will sometimes give their seats to each other. But they won't 'move up.'"

"In Denver," said Jimmie, "I once heard a conductor call out 'The gents will please step forward and the ladies set closter.' If I knew where that man was I would try to get him a position with the Metropolitan, for most of them feel as a conductor said here in New York when I jumped on him for not obeying my signal, 'Schmall bit do *I* care!'"

"Then the cars themselves," I cried, "Aren't they the most awful things! I can earnestly commend the surface cars of New York as the most awkward and uncomfortable to climb in and out of that I have ever seen. I use the word 'climb' advisedly, as the step is so high that one must take both hands to hoist oneself, while the conductor is generally obliged to reach down and seize the ambitious woman by the arm to assist her. The bell rings while you are still on the lower step; the conductor says, 'Step lively, please;' the car attains its maximum of speed at one jump; the conductor puts his dirty hand on your white silk back and gives you a forward shove, and you plunge into the nearest seat, apologizing to the people on each side of you for having sat in their laps. Then comes a cry, 'Hold fast,' and around a curve you go at a speed which throws people down, and on one occasion I saw a woman pitched from her seat.

"The Boston street railway system is the most perfect of any American city that I know of. There they pursue such a leisurely course that a Boston woman never rises from her seat until the car has come to a full stop. In fact, Bee and I were identified as strangers in town by the husband of our friend who met us at the terminus of one of the street-car lines, with his carriage. His never having seen us, and approaching us without hesitation, naturally led us to ask how he knew us. He answered:"

"'Oh, I saw you walking through the car before it reached the corner and standing on the platform when it stopped, so I said to myself, "There they are!"'"

"I can easily believe you," said Considine, "but in saying that the etiquette of any public conveyance in New York is interesting from its varieties of selfishness, oughtn't you to confine your statement to surface-cars, elevated roads, and ferry-boats, and oughtn't you to make an exception of that dignified relic of antiquity, the Fifth Avenue stage? The most uncomfortable vehicle going, yet let me give the angel his due—in a stage people do move up; everybody waits on everybody else; hands fare; rings for change, and pays all of the old-fashioned courtesies which went from a busy city life with the advent of the conductor, the autocrat of ill manners and indifference."

"Superstition evidently does not obtain in New York on one subject at least," said Aubrey, "and that is the bad luck supposing to accrue from crossing a funeral procession. Never in any other city in the world have I seen such rudeness exhibited toward the following of the dead to their last resting-place as I have seen in New York. The beautiful custom in Catholic countries not only of giving them the right of way, but of the men removing their hats while the procession passes, has resolved itself into a funeral procession going on the run; the driver of the hearse watching his chance and fairly ducking between trucks and surface-cars, jolting the casket over the tracks until I myself have seen the wreaths slip from their places, and sometimes for five or ten minutes the hearse separated from its following carriages by a procession of vehicles which the policeman at the crossing had permitted to interfere. Such a proceeding is a disgrace to our boasted civilization. We are not yet too busy nor too poor to allow our business to pause for a moment to let the solemn procession of the dead pass uninterrupted and in dignity to its last resting-place. Such consideration would permit the hearse to be driven at a reasonably slow pace in keeping with the mournful feelings of its followers. As it is now, New York funerals go at almost the pace of automobiles."

"My brother once told me," I said, "that I was so slow that some day I would get run over by a hearse. Not being an acrobat, that fate may yet overtake me in New York and yet be no disgrace to my activity."

"I am more afraid of automobiles," said Considine, shaking his head, "than I am of what I shall get in the next world. I wouldn't own one or even ride in one to save myself from hanging. I always 'screech,' as Faith says, when my cab meets one."

"You don't know how quickly they can be stopped, Considine," said Jimmie.

"That may be," retorted Considine, "but are you going to pad your broughams and put fenders on your cab horses?"

"I was in an electric cab not long ago," I said, "and a bicyclist rode daringly in front of us. In crossing the trolley-tracks, his bicycle naturally slackened a little, and my careful chauffeur brought the machine to a dead stop. Result that I was pitched out over the dashboard and barely saved myself from landing on my head.

"When I was gathered up and put back I asked the man why he stopped so suddenly (I admit that it was a foolish question, but as I am always one who asks the grocer if his eggs are fresh, I may be pardoned for this one), and he answered: 'Well, did you want me to kill that man?' I replied that of the two alternatives I would infinitely have preferred to kill the man to being killed myself,—a reply which so offended the dignity of my Jehu that he charged me double. I never did get on very well with cab-drivers."

Jimmie laughed. He was remembering the time I knocked a Paris cabman's hat off with my parasol to make him stop his cab. My methods are inclined to be a little forceful if I am frightened.

"But New York is a city of resources," I continued. "There is always somewhere to go! New York only wakes up at night and the streets present as brilliant a spectacle as Paris, for until the gray dawn breaks in the sky the streets are full of pleasure-seekers; cabs and private carriages flit to and fro; the clubs, restaurants, and supper-rooms are full to over-flowing, the lights flare, and the ceaseless whirl of America's greatest city goes on and on. And nobody ever looks bored or tired as they do in England. We are all having a good time, and we don't care who knows it. I love New York when it is time to play."

"Well, we've about done up the old town to-night," said Jimmie, as they prepared to leave. "She has hardly a leg to stand on."

"She deserves it," said Considine, gloomily. "I'm off. I'm about to desert and go back to my cabbages. New York won't let you work. She won't help you. She won't protect you. She mocks you. She laughs in your face. I'd rather die than try to work here!"

During every word of this impassioned speech the Angel and I had been growing colder and colder. We could see our-selves just where Considine had found himself—driven out of New York by reason of its abominable noise.

"And the worst of it is," went on Considine, "is that most of this noise is so unnecessary. It comes from—"

A terrific crash came from down-stairs. Three doors slammed. Then some one screamed shrilly. Considine gazed with starting eyes at the jingling globes and glasses and actually lost a little colour.

"What is it?" he whispered.

"It is nothing," said the Angel, with a wave of the hand, "but our little friends below stairs. Our neighbour is blessed with five charming little olive-branches, who have versatile tastes in athletics, and are bubbling over with animal spirits. We think privately that they are the meanest little devils that ever cursed an apartment-house, but their noise is dear to their parents, and they would not allow it when we fain would boil the children alive or beat them with bed-slats."

Jimmie laughed heartlessly, but Considine took his head between his hands.

"They have just illustrated what I was going to say. Nobody has any regard for the rights of others. Peddlers are allowed horns, and cornets, and strings of bells. Why not allow them to send up poisoned balloons to explode in your open windows, and thus call attention to their wares? I wouldn't object a bit more! Why do parents allow such noises? Have you ever remonstrated with the mother?"

"Oh, yes," said the Angel. "One day Faith called and apologized to Mrs. Gottlieb, but begged to know if she might not take the children out herself in order to let me finish a chapter. But Mrs. Gottlieb was justly incensed at any one daring to object to the healthful sports of her little brood, and said: 'Mrs. Jardine, my children are in their own apartment, and I shall allow them to make all the noise they wish.'"

"And the next day," I broke in, excitedly, "she bought the

three girls tin horns and the boys drums!"

Considine ground his teeth.

"If our wicked ways of life demanded that each of us should bear some horrible affliction, but Providence had mitigated the sentence by allowing us to choose our own form of mutilation," he said, slowly, "instead of giving up an arm or a leg or an eye, I would give up both ears and say, 'Lord, make me deaf!' For, much as I love music and the sound of my friends' voices, I believe that I could give up all conversation, and for ever deny myself to Grieg and Beethoven and Wagner rather than stand the daily, hourly torture of the street sounds of a great city."

He looked around at us and real tears stood in his eyes.

"Do you know," said the Angel, answering the look in his friend's eyes, "I believe no one on earth understands the anguish those of us who compose suffer from noise. It is not nervousness which causes us this anguish. It is the creating spirit,—the power of the man who brings words to life in literature or who brings tones to life in music. It is part of the artistic temperament, and if I ever saw a child start and shake and go white at a sudden noise, I should lay my hand on the little chap's head and say to his mother: 'Take care of that child's brain, for in it lies the power of the creator of something great. Teach him above everything self-expression that he may not labour as too many do, yet labour in vain.'"

I loved Considine for the way he looked at my Angel after that speech and the way he moved toward him and took his hand in his big, soft, strong grip.

"I can't stand it!" he declared, standing up. "I'm going. I

wouldn't live in New York if they'd give me the town. I'm going back to my five hundred acres and get in the middle of it with a revolver, and I'll shoot anything that approaches!"

But when they had all gone something like dismay seized us.

"He has so much more money than we have," I wailed, "and if *he* can't do anything where do we come in, I'd like to know!"

The Angel paced up and down thoughtfully with his hands behind his back,—an attitude conducive to deep meditation in men, I have observed.

"I think I have it," he said, finally. "Considine is too impulsive. He was not firm enough. Now I got an important letter from the agents to-day, saying that they could do nothing about the noise of the children. In the lease it expressly mentions them. I shall simply hold back the rent and see what that produces!"

I was filled with admiration at the Angel's firmness.

The result was speedily produced, such as it was. Jepson called. He called often. Then we began to get letters, and finally they threatened us with eviction. It made me feel quite Irish.

Then one day the owner and the agents and their lawyer called, and we discussed the matter. They were affable at first, but as the noise from the Gottlieb apartment grew more boisterous, their suavity departed, for they realized that our grievance was a substantial one, yet they declared they could do nothing.

"But it is in the lease," we protested. Then they delivered

themselves of what they really had come to say.

"My dear sir," said the owner, "that lease and those rules can never be enforced in this city. They simply don't hold—that's all."

"Very well," I said, triumphantly. "If the clauses upon which we took the apartment do not hold, then neither does the clause regarding the payment of the rent obtain."

They all three broke in together with hysterical eagerness:

"Ah, but that does hold. You must know that, madam."

"The rent clause is the only clause which the law backs up, is it? We have no redress against your getting us here under false pretences?"

They looked at each other uneasily. Then their masculinity asserted itself. What? To be thus browbeaten by a woman? They looked commiseratingly at the Angel for being saddled with such a wife.

They stood up to go. I looked expectantly at Aubrey.

"Gentlemen," he said, quietly. "You have heard the noises from the surrounding apartments to-day, and you have admitted that they were extraordinary. I declare them not to be borne. If then, you cannot mitigate the nuisance, this apartment will be at your disposal from the first of February."

They smiled patronizingly. The lawyer even laid his hand on the Angel's shoulder. He should have known better than that.

"My dear fellow," he said, benevolently. "You are liable for the whole year's rent—until next October. You will see by your lease."

Aubrey shook his hand off haughtily.

"Provided the lease is signed," he said, quietly. "Will you gentlemen have the goodness to find my signature on this lease? I haven't even returned it to your office."

They examined it with dropped jaws. They had not even the strength to hand it back to him. Between them it fell to the floor,—the lease whose only binding clause was the one regarding the payment of the rent.

"From the first of February," repeated the Angel, politely.

"But my dear sir," protested the lawyer, recovering first. "Let us see if we cannot adjust this little difficulty. You sign the lease, for we cannot rent such an apartment as this in midwinter. We would lose eight months' rent if you gave it up now, and I will myself personally see Mr. Gottlieb in regard to his children's noise. It really is abominable."

"We shall move this month," said Aubrey. "From the first of February this apartment is yours."

"You are very stiff about it," said the owner. "Why not be reasonable?"

"I am perfectly reasonable," said Aubrey, gently. "I have listened for an hour to the justice you administer to a tenant with a signed lease. My reason is what is guiding me now."

He rose as he spoke and moved toward the door.

They glared at us both as they went out.

Aubrey sat and figured for a few moments in silence.

"It has cost us quite a little," he said at last, "to learn that such as we cannot live in New York. We will go into the country where the right to live, and to live this side of insanity, is guaranteed, not by a lease, but by the exact centre of five acres of ground."

"I have always wanted to!" I cried, with enthusiasm. "We will be commuters."

"We will commute," said Aubrey, pausing to let the fire-engines go by, "when necessary."

# CHAPTER VIII

## MOVING

So we began our search for the Quiet Life and the spot wherein to live it. It must be out-of-town, yet not so far but that the Angel and I could get to town for an occasional feast of music or the theatre.

We asked those of our friends who were commuters to exploit the glories of their own particular towns, but to our minds there was always some insuperable objection.

So one day I took down the telephone-book and looked over the names of the towns. Jersey was tabooed on account of its mosquitoes, and both Aubrey and I cared nothing for the seashore. But the Hudson, with its beauty and the delight of its hills rising in such a profusion of loveliness back of it, seemed to draw us irresistibly.

"Anything within an hour of New York," said Aubrey.

The telephone-book should answer. I resolved to read until I got a "hunch." That is not good English, but with me it is good sense, which is better.

Finally I found a number—97 Clovertown—Bucks, Miss

Susan. Peach Orchard. The hunch was very distinct. I could fairly see my note-paper with Peach Orchard, Clovertown, stamped on it, for I instantly made up my mind that Susan must be asked to rent Peach Orchard for a term of years and go abroad. I felt sure that Europe would do her good. The more I thought of these names, the more sure I felt that we had arrived.

My next step was to look feverishly through the Clovertown names for a real estate agent. I found one, and without saying a word to the Angel, I called him up.

"Hello, Central. Give me Long Distance. Hello, Long Distance. Give me sixty-five Clovertown, please! Yes! All right. Is this Close and Murphy? Well, this is New York. I want to ask you if Peach Orchard is to let. What? I say, I would like to know if Miss Bucks would like to let Peach Orchard? She would? Well, how large is it? Four? Oh, five? Is there a good house on the place? And a stable? That's nice. I see. Yes. Well, I would like to see it to-day if I could, but it is snowing here. Not snowing there? Well, we might try. What time does a train leave 125th Street? In forty minutes? Well, my husband and I will be on that train. Oh, that's very nice. Our name is Jardine—Mr. and Mrs. Aubrey Jardine. Yes, I understand. Very well. Good-bye."

I hung up the receiver, and rushed into the dining-room.

"Hurry with luncheon, Aubrey!" I said. "I've rented a place in Clovertown, and we go out to take possession to-day. We leave in forty minutes!"

Aubrey looked up with interest.

"I heard you at the telephone. You are a crazy little cat," he said, but I could see that he was charmed. We love to do crazy things.

"He's going to meet us at the station with a carriage," I explained as I struggled into my coat with Mary's help, and Aubrey pawed madly around in the dark closet for overshoes for both of us.

Mary flew about like a distracted hen until she saw us safely started. Most people would have gone mad at our erratic proceedings, but nothing ever disturbed Mary's equanimity. In fact, crises fairly delighted her. In an emergency she rose to the heights of Napoleon.

Finally we started, caught the train, and arrived. The gallant Mr. Close met us, true to his word, and in five minutes we were on our way to Peach Orchard.

As we drove into the grounds, Mr. Close clapped his hand to his forehead with an exclamation.

"What is it?" I said, with a sinking heart.

"I've forgotten the key!"

"Never mind," I said, blithely. "We can easily get in through a window. My husband used to be a burglar."

It never occurred to me that the poor man would take such an idiotic remark seriously, so we neither of us looked at him until we had examined every door and window to find if haply one had been left unlocked. Nor did we notice that we were doing all the work until Aubrey selected the back hall window as the loosest, and opening his knife—the wickedest looking pocket-knife I ever saw, by the way—he proceeded deftly to turn the lock of the window and then to raise it.

I was so proud of his cleverness that I turned to ensure the admiration of Mr. Close also, but the look I encountered froze the smile on my lips and the words on my tongue, for the good man was viewing both Aubrey and me with the liveliest horror and distrust.

Aubrey turned also at my sudden silence, and the light dawned upon us both in the same instant.

Mr. Close had the grace to look quite sheepish to see us both sit down abruptly on the top step and shriek with laughter. But I am sure, in my own mind, that he dismissed the idea of burglars in favour of lunatics.

But Peach Orchard was well named, for the old house was set down in the very midst of it. Trees were everywhere, and, indeed, they grew so close to the house, and they were so tall, that we could not see the house properly. The short winter afternoon was drawing to a close and it looked for a moment as if we would have to come again, when on a shelf, good Mr. Close, whose business instincts were keener than his sense of humour, found an old lamp with about three inches of oil in it. A feverish search for matches resulted in the discovery that his match-box was empty, and Aubrey's held only one.

Right here, let me ask just one question of all the smokers all over the world. Why is it, that, needing them more than you need anything else on earth,—home or friends or wife or mother or money or position or religion or your hope of heaven,—why is it that you never have any matches?

Aubrey's one, which he had been saving, as he told me afterward, to light a cigarette on the return drive, proved friendly, and the lamp smoked instead. Armed with this rather unsatisfactory torch, we explored, and as we went up and down, in and out of the queer old place, built a hundred years ago (Mr. Close said!), we decided to take it, and most unwisely said so, thereby paying, as usual, the top price for something which we could have got at a bargain if we had waited. But such is the perennial foolishness and precipitancy of the Jardines.

Evidently Mary had humoured our going out to Clovertown that afternoon as one of our mad excursions only, and had not fathomed the possibility of our deciding to live there, for when we came home and gaily announced that we had rented Peach Orchard, Mary's jaw fell and her lip pouted sulkily.

This lasted during dinner. We could both see that she intended us to notice it and question her, and when the coffee had been served and we said she might go, she saw that she must open the ball herself, so she fingered her apron and said:

"Missis, I shall be sorry not to go with you to Clovertown, but of all the towns along the Hudson, that is the one I can't bear to go to!"

"Why, Mary?" I said, for the first time in my life suspecting her of the tricks which we afterward came to know were a part of her.

"Because my oldest sister was killed by the railroad right at the station at Clovertown, and I was the one to take her away!"

For about the ten thousandth time Mary held the trump. I felt crushed. I could fairly picture the scene, and I knew that no one could face such harrowing memories. As I gazed at her and she saw I was touched, tears began to gather in her eyes, brim over and run down her pink cheeks. I felt fairly faint and sick to think of parting with Mary.

Then something told me to probe the matter.

"When was your sister killed, Mary?" I said.

"Just twenty-two years ago come Washington's Birthday, Missis dear," whimpered Mary, with her apron at her eye.

I began to laugh heartlessly.

"And wasn't that the sister you fought with and hated—the one you have told me a dozen times you were glad to know was dead?" I went on.

Mary nodded, rather sheepishly. I saw she was weakening, so I became firm.

"Now, Mary," I said, and it was the first time I ever had spoken sternly to her, "put that apron down, and don't let me hear another word about your not going to Clovertown. Of course you are going! Any grief, no matter what, could be cured in twenty-two years,—let alone a grief which never was a grief. And you did *not* see her after she was dead—you told me you wouldn't go. And what made you the maddest was having to pay the funeral expenses when she had a husband who could have paid them if he would only work. So now, you can just stop those onion tears," I said, marching haughtily toward the door, followed somewhat sheepishly by the Angel, who longed to turn back and mitigate my sternness.

The longing finally conquered him.

"Besides, Mary," he said, pacifically, turning back at the door, "we couldn't possibly get along without you. You are absolutely necessary to us. Who, I ask you, would do up my white waistcoat and duck trousers if *you* left?"

Mary beamed at this seductive flattery, and bridled visibly.

"Tell me all about it, Boss dear," she said.

And in so doing she and we both forgot that she had suggested going, and nothing more was ever said about it.

Seldom can I look back, however, and recall an instance when we obtained more feverish and thrilling joy than from those next few days when we mentally improved and furnished Peach Orchard.

With what excitement did we lay rugs and place furniture in our mind's eye! How we appealed frantically to each other to decide whether there were three or four windows in the library, and with what complacency did we discover that, owing to a shrewd forethought of my own in furnishing the smoking and living rooms in our apartment with similar curtains, we now had enough for the great, light, airy sitting-room at Peach Orchard.

Then we took a long breath and fell with fresh avidity into the subject of improvements. Mr. Close was of the opinion that Susan would do nothing—could do nothing rather, as she had a consumptive brother who must live in the Adirondacks, and her resources were few. Therefore, we recklessly decided that if she would give us an option on the place for another year, we would make the improvements ourselves. Fools!

Yet why fools! Never have we so enjoyed spending money, and as Anthony Hope says that "economy is going without something you want, for fear that sometime you'll want something which probably you won't want," we felt upheld and strengthened in the knowledge that we were never, by any means, economical.

But the Angel was prospering. Those who frankly predicted that we would starve or be divorced were now glad to sit at our well-set table and smoke the Angel's good cigars and sip his excellent wines. And feeling that we might branch out a *little*, we promptly branched out a great deal, and nearly went to smash in consequence.

But God watches over children and fools, and we were saved, and sped upon our way in a manner so like a special dispensation of Providence that no lesson was learned to teach us to be more careful next time. In fact, it encouraged us in our recklessness, for in our darkest hour the Angel's first play was accepted, and, being staged, was so instantaneously a success that he gave up novels altogether and began to devote himself to the drama. He devoted to it, I mean to say, all the time he could spare from the improving of Peach Orchard.

Those days, the first of our prosperity and the first of our housekeeping in a real house, were the happiest we had ever known. Susan had been persuaded to let the place for a term of years with an option to buy, so we felt as if we owned it already. But that is a peculiarity of the Jardines.

We tore out the old plumbing, we put in two new bathrooms. We made a laundry out of the storeroom. We cut doors and threw rooms together which never had associated before, and we turned all the windows which gave upon the porches into doors, so that we could step out-of-doors at will. We ordered our porch screened entirely, and planned to furnish it as a study for Aubrey. We put paper-hangers, painters, gas, telephone, and electric men at work all over the house, and made them promise, yea, even swear, to finish their work by a certain time.

But, having, as we thought, learned wisdom by experience, we put no faith in their promises, but engaged Mr. Close in person to go every day to superintend things.

As the day drew near to move we became most agitated as to ways and means. It seemed a gigantic task to crate and barrel everything and move from one town to another, and while we discussed hiring a car, Mary interrupted.

"Excuse me, Boss and Missis dear, for putting in my two cents, but you surely aren't thinking of sending all the furniture by freight, when vans are so much more convenient?"

"Vans?" we cried. "Will vans move us thirty miles?"

"Fifty, if you like," said Mary, promptly.

"From one town to another?"

"From one State to another, and without taking the pins out of the cushions or the sugar out of the bowls."

At once the idea of the sugar-bowls and pincushions fascinated me. I begged Aubrey to investigate, and he agreed with enthusiasm to do it the very next day.

"If I might suggest," said Mary again, "all Boss will have to do is to telephone to two or three different companies to come and estimate the cost. He won't have to run after 'em any farther than the telephone."

We followed her suggestion, and to our delight discovered

that all she said was true and more. They agreed to insure against breakage, thieves, and fire; to pack all the stuff in vans one day, take them to their warehouse for the early part of the night, and start at one o'clock for Clovertown,— agreeing to make the whole distance, unload, place the furniture, and unpack the china before leaving that night.

We need not lift a hand. All we had to do was to go to a hotel for one night, and take a train for Clovertown the next morning.

It was almost too easy. I reflected what "moving" meant to people who live in small towns where such conveniences do not exist. Verily, New York might be noisy, but she was a city of superb conveniences. Only Paris excels her in her purveying shops, for in Paris one can buy the wing of a chicken only, and that just around the corner, while in New York one must buy at least the whole fowl (and pay the price of a house and lot in Louisville, let me pause to remark!), but in justice I must also add that such luxuries are also "just around the corner."

By implicitly following Mary's advice we saw everything safely placed in the vans and move majestically from our door. Then we betook ourselves to the Waldorf, with our "glad rags," as Jimmie had commanded, in our suit-cases, and dined in state, and went to Weber and Fields afterward. Jimmie wanted me to hear Weber persuade Lillian Russell to invest in oil.

Now at that, the Angel and Mrs. Jimmie simply smiled indulgently. While Jimmie and I reeled in our seats and clutched each other's sleeves and shrieked (in as ladylike a manner as we could), while tears poured down our cheeks and our ribs cramped and our breath failed. That is the way Jimmie and I enjoy things. That is also why we can stand it to travel in the same party, and not come home hating each other.

But all the time, even in the midst of the fun, my mind turned lovingly toward the warehouse where our precious furniture reposed, safely packed in those huge red vans.

Jimmie noticed my preoccupation, and said:

"If you could take your mind off coal-scuttles long enough, I would like to ask you what you thought of Prince Henry? Aubrey says you met him last week."

"We did, we met him the same day we bought the ice-box," I answered.

"Ye gods!" growled Jimmie, in deep disgust. "Think of remembering a royal prince by the day you bought the ice-box!"

"What most impressed you, dear?" inquired Mrs. Jimmie, sweetly.

"The price!" I answered, cheerfully. "It was a slightly damaged article, so we got it for less than half the original cost of it. You know I do love a bargain, Mrs. Jimmie."

"I meant the prince, dear," said Mrs. Jimmie.

"However, if she prefers to discuss ice-boxes," said Jimmie, politely, "by all means, let us bring the conversation down to her level. It will not be the first time I have had to do it."

"I don't care!" I said, stoutly. "It was far more interesting than seeing the prince. This, you must remember, was our *first* ice-box. The other one was built into the apartment, and we didn't own it."

"I do wish Bee could hear you!" jeered Jimmie. "Gee, but you will be a trial to Bee."

"I always have been," I said. "She got mad at me just before I was married about a thing as foolish as anything *I* ever heard of. I had calls to pay, and I asked Bee to go with me. She said she'd go if I'd get a carriage, so I said I would, and told her to order it. But it seems that all the good ones were engaged for a funeral, and they sent us a one-horse brougham with the driver not in livery. We didn't notice it until we opened the front door. Then Bee sailed in. 'Why are you not in livery?' she demanded. 'I shall certainly report you to Mr. Overman. He ought to be ashamed to send out a driver without a livery!' 'If you please, ma'am,' said the man, 'I'm Mr. Overman, and rather than disappoint you ladies, as all my men are out, I thought I'd drive you myself.' Well, that was too much for even Bee. So she thanked him, and in we got. The first house we went to was that of a haughty society dame of whose opinion Bee stood much in awe. Personally, I thought her an illiterate old bore. She was newly rich, and laid great emphasis upon such things as maids' caps, while tucking her own napkin under her chin at dinner. She followed us to the door in an excess of cordiality which amused me, considering everything, and there, to our horror, we saw poor old Overman half-way under the horse, examining one of its hoofs! Poor Bee! I gave one look at her face and giggled. That was enough. She was so enraged that she wouldn't pay another call. She took me straight home as if I were a bad child, and the next day I paid my calls alone."

"And yet," said Jimmie, musingly, "can you or any of us ever forget the night that Bee did the skirt dance in Tyrol?"

"Dear Bee!" said Mrs. Jimmie, softly. "How charming she is!"

"Yet she wouldn't approve of your going to Clovertown," said Jimmie. "She hates the bucolic. Idyls and pastorals are not in it with our rue de la Paix Bee. I'll bet she will never come to see you at Peach Orchard."

"Let us hope for the best," said Aubrey. "It is dangerous to prophesy."

"We're going to keep a cow, Jimmie!" I said, rapturously.

"Well, don't gurgle about it. You act as if keeping a cow put the stamp of the Four Hundred on you. Did Mary say you might?"

"Mary has given her consent," said Aubrey. "But I'm wondering how that old woman will behave with other servants. Of course she was all right while there was no one else and she was boss of the ranch, but we must have two or three now at Peach Orchard, and she is so jealous, I wonder if she will let us live with her!"

Well might we have wondered. Trouble began the very next day. As we went out on the train I noticed that Mary had on her best dress and hat. She had no bag with her, so I wondered how she meant to "settle" in such clothes. The Angel and I had on our worst.

I comforted myself with the reflection that there would not be very much dirty work to do. This would in reality be a kid-glove moving, for Mr. Close had telephoned the day before that everything was ready for us to move in. I had even sent a cleaning woman for floors and windows.

I had taken the precaution to bring a few silver knives, forks, and spoons in my bag. Then as we got off the train I stopped at a grocery and bought a loaf of bread, a tin of devilled ham, one of sardines, some butter, and a dozen eggs, so we were at least sure of our luncheon.

We jumped out of the carriage almost before it had stopped, and, while Aubrey paid the man, I ran up the steps and into the house.

Such a sight of confusion met my eyes! The old paper was piled in the middle of each floor, and not a new strip on any wall. One ceiling only in the whole house was finished. Not a hardwood floor had been laid. The lumber was piled in the hall. Not a chandelier was up. The ragged wires projected from their various holes in ceilings and walls. Where was my cleaning woman? Where were our workmen? Above all, where was the perfidious Mr. Close?

There was no furnace fire, and the water was not turned on. I ran back and Aubrey shouted for the carriage, just turning out of the grounds, to come back.

"Go to the plumbers!" I said, incoherently, "and to the electric light men, and to the agents, and see where the men are, and bring some brooms and buckets and send me a grocer's boy."

He turned away, breathing vengeance. I felt sorry for Mr. Close.

"And to the telephone company!" I cried, after the departing carriage.

"And to—" but the driver lashed his horses, and I had to give up.

I went back to Mary in her best dress.

"Finished, is it?" she said, sniffing with indignation. "I suppose the agent thought we were flies, and could move in on the ceiling—as that's the only thing I can see about the house that's finished!"

"Wait until Mr. Jardine sees the agent!" I said, ominously. "Then something else will be finished, besides the ceiling."

"I hope he'll kill him!" said Mary, pleasantly.

It was a real pleasure to witness the dismay in Mr. Close's face when Aubrey returned, bringing him, mentally, by the scruff of the neck. I have seen terriers yanked back to look at things they have "worried" in much the same manner that Mr. Close was fetched to Peach Orchard.

"Just look, Mr. Close, if you please," I said, ominously polite. "You telephoned me yesterday and said you had been here personally and seen with your own eyes that everything was finished and the house in perfect readiness for us to move in."

Mr. Close refused to meet my accusing eye. He turned green.

There are more ways than one of calling a man a liar. And some are safer than others.

"Did you really have the smoke test put through the plumbing as you said you did?" I asked.

Mr. Close eagerly produced the bill.

Plumber's bills are conclusive evidence.

"Did you have the range cleaned and the water-back examined?" demanded Aubrey.

Mr. Close swore that he did. Aubrey led him captive around the house and showed him the confusion thereof, Mary grimly following. I think Close preferred Aubrey to me, and me or anybody to Mary, for Mary's very spectacles were bristling with anger. She could see herself, in her best dress, having to clean up that mess so that the furniture could be moved in.

Then Aubrey's men began to arrive. The man with the chandeliers. The carpenters to lay the floors. The man from the water office. My negro cleaning woman and the grocer's boy. Fortunately, the cleaning woman had brought a broom, a mop, and a bucket.

As there were no fires, Aubrey and Mr. Close made one in the furnace; Mary and the grocer's boy—or rather the grocer's boy under Mary's direction—built one in the range, while I set the woman to sweeping one floor for the carpenters to begin on.

Suddenly I heard hurried feet running up the cellar stairs. The water man had turned the water on from the street, and it was gaily pouring into the cellar. Mr. Close is a fat man, but he ran like a jack-rabbit to that water main, and shut it off. Then without daring to face—Mary, he started to town for a plumber.

He had not been gone half an hour when the water-back blew up. Fortunately, no one was in the kitchen at the time, but the cleaning woman turned from black to a dirty gray with fright, and without further ado went home. I can't say that I blamed her. Aubrey was busy putting out the furnace fire and bailing out the cellar, so he did not know of that defection.

However, a culmination of such calamities, instead of smiting me to the earth, aroused every drop of fighting blood in my whole body.

I went out on the porch to think it over, and as I thought I began to laugh. I laughed until Aubrey heard me and thought I was crying. He came hurrying out, with a face full of anxiety, saying, before he saw me:

"Never mind, dear! I know this is hard on you, but—"

"Well, I'll be—!"

Both of those remarks were Aubrey's. He was much relieved, however, to discover that I was not cast down by all these disasters. In fact, our moving partook more of the delights of camping out than orthodox housekeeping, and I soon discovered expedients.

The only fire which did not bid fair to blow our heads off was one in the grate in the hall. On this we boiled water and made tea, and for that first luncheon we satisfied ourselves with sardines and devilled ham sandwiches. But as we were obliged to cook on that grate for six days, I may as well record now that we grew into expert cooks, attempting eggs in all forms, batter-cakes, hoe cakes, fried mush, bacon, ham, chops, toast, and fried potatoes,—in fact, no woman knows how much she can cook on a common little hard coal grate until three hungry people are dependent on it for three meals a day.

We supplemented this by the chafing-dish. Aubrey says that I should say the grate fire supplemented the chafing-dish, for nobody knows what can be done with one—in real, urgent housekeeping, I mean, such as ours, until one has tried. It makes a perfect double boiler, and as for a *bain Marie*, well,

I used to cream potatoes in the top part, and when they were all done but the simmering of the cream to thicken it, I used to put tomatoes in the bottom part to stew, and put the potato part back on the tomatoes for a cover and to keep hot. Did you ever try that?

The kitchen range was discovered to be ruined, the pipes being completely full and solid with rust. It is a miracle that some of us were not killed by the explosion. Mary cheerfully declared her regret that Mr. Close had not been bending over the stove with his lie in his throat when the water-back remonstrated. Mary is quite firm in her ideas of making "the punishment fit the crime—the punishment fit the crime."

But we enjoyed it—that is, Aubrey and I enjoyed it. Mary wanted us to go to an hotel and stay until things were in order, and send the bill to Mr. Close. But even though her suggestion was made at two o'clock in the afternoon and no vans had yet appeared, I was firm in my decision to sleep in Peach Orchard that night.

My courage had in the meantime been buoyed up by the fact that the telephone had been put in, and my friend, the grocer's boy, had brought me reinforcements in the shape of plates, tumblers, pots, pans, brooms, buckets, and supplies, and had further completed my rapture by promising me a kitten.

About three o'clock, I, as lookout, descried the big red vans, each drawn by four horses, at the foot of the hill.

Now Clovertown is not full of hills, rather it consists of hills. It is not quite as bad as Mt. St. Michel, for that is all one, but Clovertown consists of a series of small Mt. St. Michels, equally steep, precipitous, and appalling to climb, also equally lovely and bewitching when once you have climbed.

The moving men seemed to realize their steepness, for they put all eight of the horses to one van and bravely started up the hill. But alas, they were New York horses, and only capable of dodging elevated pillars and of keeping their footing on icy asphalt. They were not used to climbing trees, as we afterward discovered Clovertown horses to be quite capable of doing. So, after straining and pulling and being cruelly urged to a feat beyond their strength, we had our first taste of the neighbourliness of the people on the next estate. Their head man, called familiarly Eddie Bannon, came to our rescue.

"Take all them horses off," he said, "and I'll pull you up the hill with my team of blacks."

We were grateful, but politely incredulous. What! One pair of horses accomplish a feat which eight had been unable to do.

I grew feverishly excited in watching the exchange. It was a picture to see the incredulity on the countenances of the van men. They tried not to show it, for that would have been impolite, but Eddie Bannon saw it, and grinned at their unbelief.

When the blacks were in the traces, Bannon took the reins. One of the men offered him a long wicked-looking whip, but he spurned it.

"No," he said, "if the blacks won't pull for love, they won't for a beating."

So then he spoke to them. Willing hands started the wheels. The gallant little blacks, looking like a pair of ponies before the huge van, seemed to lie flat on their bellies as they strained forward, digging their sharp little hoofs into the hillside. The van gave an inch—two! A foot! Then urged by their master's voice, and for very pride of home and race and breed, the gallant blacks pulled for dear life, and in a quarter of an hour the van was at our door, and they were switching their tails and stamping their hoofs and shaking their intelligent heads in the pride of victory.

As for Bannon, he stroked and praised them in an ecstasy of self-vindication, and was refusing the van man's offer to buy them at "a hundred dollars apiece more than they cost."

Those horses pulled our three vans up our hill, if you will believe it, and seemed rather to enjoy the grind they had on the other horses, so that, in a fever of appreciation, I had to go and feed apples and sugar to all ten of them, and to remind the blacks that the New York horses had been pulling those vans since midnight, all of which I begged them to take into consideration, while not in the least depreciating their own glorious achievement.

The initiated need not be told how, when hardwood floors are being laid, furniture is moved from room to room to accommodate the carpenters, and the uninitiated will not be interested at the recital. It must be experienced to be appreciated.

We lived through it. We learned not to object when the ice-box was set up in the hall so near the grate that the drip-pan had to be emptied every hour, and the iceman had to come twice a day. We learned to step over rolls of rugs and to bark our shins on rocking-chairs and to trip over hidden objects with only a pleasant smile.

We screened one porch entirely, and furnished it as a study for Aubrey. We had now papered and painted the house from top to bottom. We had put in gas, telephone, and electric light, and when we could no longer think of any further way to spend money, we turned our attention to the garden.

I longed for old Amos, my uncle's gardener and coachman in Louisville. His experience would be invaluable, and as the estate had been divided and no one had any use for the old grizzled negro, they let me have him. I adored Amos. It was he who had attended to all my childish pleasures on the plantation when I went there to visit, and, in turn, he thought "Miss Faith honey" could do no wrong. It is a comfort to have some one in one's childish memory who thinks one can do no wrong, even if it is only a servant.

So old Amos came and made flower-beds, and persuaded us to buy a pair of horses in addition to the one we had hitherto modestly used, and thus, with the aid of friends' and judicious servants' advice, we were by way of being landed proprietors, and came to look upon Peach Orchard as an estate.

Then the grocer's boy gave me the promised kitten, a common tiger kitten, which we named Mitnick, and soon afterward we acquired not only one cow, but several, our especial pride being an imported Guernsey, which figures quite prominently in my narrative further on. And as Aubrey's unwonted prosperity continued, we endeavoured not to let our riches increase too fast, by spending every cent upon which we could lay our hands on the place. But who, who owns a country place, can help it? Or who would help it if he could?

We raised our own flowers and vegetables regardless of expense. We could have ordered American Beauties from New York every day for what our hollyhocks and clove pinks and common annuals cost us. We planted five bushels of potatoes and dug three and a half, which made them come to a dollar a bushel more than if we had bought them at the grocer's. And as to our milk and cream—I once heard the Angel say to Jimmie when they came out for a visit:

"Which will you have, old man? A glass of champagne or a glass of milk? They both cost the same!"

But what of it? Weren't they *our* cows which gave the milk? And weren't they *our* potatoes which rotted in the ground, and *our* chickens which died before we could kill them? It was the pride of ownership which ate into our lives and made us quite sickening to our friends whose tastes ran to pink teas and hotel verandas, while we, poor fools, lived each day nearer to the soil, and loved more dearly the earth which nourished us.

# CHAPTER IX

## HOW BEE TRIED TO MAKE US SMART

Bee had spent nearly all the time since we were married in Europe, and had never, therefore, paid the Angel and me a visit. But this very afternoon she was to arrive.

The arrival of one's sister need not necessarily mean anything as alarming as a smallpox scare, but if you knew the somewhat revolutionary methods, adopted with a ladylike quiet and a well-bred calm, which characterize Bee's visits to her relatives, you would excuse our somewhat flurried preparations to entertain her. In addition to our natural desire to do our best for her, Bee had sent a letter clearly setting forth the style of entertainment she expected of us, and indicating that no paltry excuses would be taken for our not coming up to her wishes.

Aubrey was at first for open rebellion.

"If she will take us as she finds us, Bee will be welcome to come and stay as long as she likes," he said, while her letter was still fresh in our minds.

"She won't," I said, with conviction. Bee is my sister, or to speak more accurately, I am Bee's sister. "She will come prepared to make radical changes in our mode of living, in everything from our religion to the way we have hung the pictures."

Aubrey used one small unprintable word.

"Furthermore," I added, "she will be so smooth and plausible about it, that you will not object to carrying out her wishes."

The Angel gave me a look.

"If we carry out her wishes, do you think that will be the reason?" he asked, quietly.

"No," I cried, impulsively. "It will be because as a host or as anything else you are an Angel."

But he is also a diplomat, as his next remark will show.

"As we are incapable with such generic instructions," he said, tapping Bee's letter with his pipe, "of knowing just how we must make ourselves over to suit her, and as Bee is never quite happy unless she is managing other people's affairs, suppose we wait until she comes and gives us specific orders?"

This was what I considered the height, climax, and acme of hospitality.

"Only," he warned me as we drove to the station to meet her, "try to remain, within bounds. The only thing I ha—criticize about Bee is that she makes such a coward of you. Remember when she tries to browbeat you, that *I* consider your taste and common sense better than hers, and that in any stand you take I am back of you, no matter what it is."

I pressed the Angel's hand gratefully. Bee's train was appallingly near, and my blissful married independence was rapidly degenerating into my former state of jelly-like sisterly dependence.

Bee is one of those persons who, consciously or unconsciously, make you feel the moment you meet her the difference between your clothes and hers. I had almost forgotten this, but the second she stepped from the train I was invisibly informed of the distance between us. I had put on my best, and Aubrey said I looked very well, but in Bee's first sweeping glance at me I felt sure that my dress was wrong in the back.

The carriage drove up, and, as Bee stepped into it, I noticed, that the horses were too fat, and that, while old Uncle Amos might be a comfort, he certainly was not stylish. I never had thought of these things before.

In other words, Bee brought the city into too close juxtaposition for the country to enjoy without a Mark-Tapley effort to come out strong under trying circumstances.

Our place, Peach Orchard, was old, rambling, and picturesque. But it was also comfortable. Both the Angel and I hate the idea of pioneering or of doing without city comforts. So we had put bathrooms in here and electric lights there, and, by adding city improvements to a country estate, we had made of Peach Orchard a dear old place. It was a place, too, over which some people raved, so I was loth to view it through my critical sister's eyes for fear of permanent disenchantment.

But at first Bee was very polite. She affected an interest in the cows and the number of hens sitting and how many more chickens we got than the people whose estate adjoins. She spoke of the butter, which so filled me with enthusiasm that I sent down to the dairy and had Mary bring up Katie's last churning to show her. I was so interested in the colour of the golden rolls in their cheese-cloth coverings that I did not notice Bee's expression until afterward.

At five Bee asked for tea. There were some hurried whispered instructions before we got it. But we pulled through that all right.

Then Bee said:

"Who is coming out to-night?"

"Coming out where?" I asked, genially.

"Why, to dine. Surely, you don't dine here alone, just you two, every evening?"

I looked at Aubrey, and he looked at me.

"To be sure we do! Do you think we are already so bored by each other that we send to New York for people to amuse us?" I cried, with some spirit.

"Oh, not at all!" answered Bee, politely. "Only, I thought perhaps, now that I am here, you would have some one from town for me to talk to."

"Why, I'll talk to you and so will Aubrey—"

I stopped in confusion. Again it was something in Bee's expression, I felt the same way when I called her attention to the length of the sorrels' tails. It reminded me that Bee preferred them docked.

"It is your first night with us, so nobody will be here to-night," I said, rising to the emergency. "But to-morrow we'll have somebody. I'll ask the Jimmies!"

"Or perhaps you could get Captain Featherstone from Fort Hamilton," suggested Bee.

"That is not likely," I said. "He has so many engagements."

"You might try him—by telephone," suggested Bee again.

"Certainly, I'll ask him," I said, cordially.

Aubrey pressed my handkerchief into my hand with a meaning twinkle in his eyes, and when Bee went in to dress, he said:

"It will be rather nice to see old Featherstone again, don't you think?"

"Yes, if we can get him," I answered.

"You poor little goose," said Aubrey, "don't you know they have it all arranged, and that Featherstone won't go beyond earshot of the telephone until he receives your invitation?"

To be sure! I had forgotten Bee's methods.

Of course it turned out as Aubrey predicted—it always does. Captain Featherstone accepted with suspicious alacrity.

For three days Bee was polite, and I, who am most easily gulled for a person who looks as intelligent as I do, was pluming myself upon the fact that our modest mode of living was proving agreeable to Bee's jaded European palate. I wondered if she had noticed my housekeeping. She had not expressed herself in any way, but I wondered if she had observed how scrupulously neat everything was, that there was no lint on the floors and what bully things we had to eat.

I was the more eager to know what she thought from the fact that most of my friends had not hesitated to say that I couldn't keep house, and the Angel would starve. And once when I wrote home for a recipe for tomato soup and one of the girls heard of it, she actually sent me this insulting telegram: "Tomato soup! You! O Lord!"

Which just shows you.

So, on the third day, on seeing Bee cast a critical look around, I said, unable to wait another minute for the praises I was sure would come:

"Well, what do you think of us anyway?"

Then I leaned back with the thought in my mind, "Now here is where, as Jimmie would say, I get a bunch of hot air."

Bee wheeled around on me eagerly, and I smiled in anticipation.

"Do you really want to know?"

"Of course I do!" I cried, impatiently.

"You asked me, you know," she said, warningly.

"I know I did. Go ahead. Tell me."

"Tell you what I think of you?" said Bee, looking me over as if to find a sensitive spot for her blow to fall on. "Well, I think that you are the most hopelessly *bourgeoise* mortal I ever knew."

I sat up.

"*Bourgeois!*" I exploded.

"From a woman with social possibilities," she went on, "you have degenerated into a mere housewife. And you and Aubrey have become positively—"

She paused in order to be more impressive.

"Domestic!" she hissed at last with such vehemence that I bit my tongue. As I put in no defence she went on, gathering momentum as she talked.

"When I heard that you had come to live in one of the smartest towns along the Hudson, where millionaires are as thick as blackberries, I said to myself: 'Now they will rise to the occasion.' But have you? No! I come, fresh from those gorgeous house-parties in England, to find you and Aubrey no better than farmers and—satisfied with yourselves! If you could only get my point of view and see *how* satisfied you are!"

"We are happy,—that's what it is!" I interpolated, feebly.

"Then be miserable, but progress!" cried Bee. "Such a state of social stagnation as you exist in is a sin against yours and Aubrey's talents."

I was so stunned I forgot to bow at this unexpected compliment.

"Here you are in the midst of smart traps, servants in livery, horses with docked tails and magnificent harnesses, perfectly contented with fat, lazy horses, an old negro coachman in a green coat, and carriages whose simplicity is simply disgusting. There is only one really magnificent thing about Peach Orchard, and that is the dog."

I felt faint. To have earned the right to live in Bee's eyes only by a dog's breadth! It was mortifying.

"I don't care so much for myself," pursued Bee, comfortably, "but what Sir Wemyss and Lady Lombard will say, *I* don't know."

"Why, they aren't coming here, are they?" I gasped, sitting up.

"They are, if you will invite them. Of course I have nowhere to entertain them, in return for all they did for me, and I thought possibly you would ask them here for a fortnight, but since I have seen how you live—unless, perhaps, you would be willing to be smartened up a bit?"

Bee looked distinctly hopeful.

"What would you suggest?" I asked, huskily.

Bee cleared her throat in a pleased way.

"First of all, let me be assured that I will not be embarrassing you," she said, politely. "You can afford to—to branch out a little?"

"Yes," I said. But my pleasure in the admission was not keen.

"Then," said Bee, "I would advise a coachman and a footman in livery. I know just where two excellent Englishmen can be got. Then you want all this made into lawns. You want to exercise the horses more, and have their tails docked. And above all you want a victoria."

"We have got that," I said. "I was going to surprise you with it. It came this morning."

"Where is it?" cried Bee, standing up and shaking out her gown.

"In the barn, but perhaps—"

"Let's go and look at it!" exclaimed Bee. Then as we started she laid her hand kindly on my arm. "And please say 'stables,' not 'barn.' Sir Wemyss might not know what you meant."

I giggled at this, for ours is so hopelessly a barn. Nobody but a fool would try to rejuvenate the huge red structure by the word "stables." It sheltered the lovely, soft-eyed Jerseys, a score of sitting hens in one retired corner, the horses, the feed, the carriages, and farm implements. Stables indeed!

Bee walked straight by all the animals, who turned their heads and gave me a welcome after their several kinds, and stood in delighted contemplation before the beautiful shining victoria.

"That is a beauty!" she said, at length. "Aubrey certainly knows what's what, even if you don't. Now I can tell you what has been in my mind all day long. Oh, do leave that cow alone and listen! Call the dog!"

Jack, our snow-white bulldog, came at a word. Bee beamed on him.

"It is the latest—the very latest fad in London to drive in a victoria with a white bulldog on the seat with you!" she said, complacently. "And Jack will be simply perfect for the part."

"Shall I train Aubrey to run behind with his tongue hanging out, in Jack's place?" I asked.

"Now there you go—rejecting my simplest suggestion!" cried Bee. "My simplest, my smartest, and my least expensive! This won't cost you a penny, and it will attract attention at once."

I closed my eyes for a moment to contemplate just what sort of attention we would attract if the dog and I drove to the Station to meet Aubrey.

"Suppose we try it now!" suggested Bee. "Will you have Amos bring out the horses?"

Bee is always scrupulously polite about not giving orders to my servants direct, although I have begged her to consider them as her own. I always think that a hostess who neglects to make her guests feel at liberty to give an order either is not accustomed to servants or else stands in too much awe of them.

Jack, the bulldog, assisted in our preparations with much getting under our feet and many hearty tail-waggings. Little he knew what was to follow!

Bee carefully gave me my position at the right, and took her own.

"Now," she said, "there are two equally correct ways of sitting in a victoria, neither of which you are doing."

I was quite comfortable, but I immediately sat up.

"It depends upon what you have on," Bee proceeded. "If you are tailor-made and it is morning, you sit straight like this. If it is afternoon and you are all of a Parisian fluff, you recline like this and put your feet as far out on the cushion as you can. It shows off your instep."

"It comes very near showing off your garter," I said, indignantly. "You needn't expect me to lie down like that and put my feet on the coachman's back. Aubrey would have a fit."

"You are positively low," said Bee, straightening herself. I giggled helplessly at her instructions. They were so beyond my power to carry them out properly.

"Can't I sit like this? Can't I be comfortable? What's a victoria for, anyhow?" I demanded.

"Call the dog!" was Bee's only answer.

I called him. He came to the step, his tongue hanging out, his stumpy tail wagging.

"What'll you have, girls?" he seemed to say.

"Get in here! Come up, Jack!" I coaxed, patting the seat invitingly.

Jack put one paw on the step, and wagged his tail harder. Old Amos's shoulders shook.

"Don' reckon you all will git dat dorg into de kerredge, Miss Faith," he said. "Look lake he smell a trick."

It certainly did look as if he smelled treachery, for nothing could persuade him to enter our chariot. Finally the stable-boy lifted him bodily. Bee seized a paw and I his two ears, and thus protesting we dragged him to a position between us. He was badly frightened by such treatment, but remembering that I had been his friend in times past, his tail fluttered amiably. I gave a hurried order to Amos to drive out quickly, but as the carriage began to move, Jack's big body trembled violently, and he lifted up his voice in a howl of protest which woke the echoes. He tried to jump out, but as both Bee and I had our arms around him, more in anxiety than affection, however, he realized that we desired his society, and forbore to escape. Jack is a good deal of a gentleman, you see, albeit primitive in his methods of showing his discomfort.

"He'll soon stop," said Bee, encouragingly. "He feels strange at first."

But he didn't stop. The more familiar his surroundings became, the more we passed horses and dogs he knew, the keener became his humiliation at driving by in enervating luxury, where once he had trotted pantingly in the dust and heat. His howl changed to a deep bay, and the bay to a long-drawn wailing, which was so full of pain that the passers-by made audible comments. As for me, I was afraid every moment that we would be arrested by a member of the S. P. C. A., but fortunately the populace seemed to think we were on our way to the veterinary surgeon for a dangerous operation.

"Poor fellow!" said one, "you can see he is injured by the way they are holding him!"

"Ain't them ladies kind-hearted now to take that ugly-lookin' old bulldog in that fine carriage to the doctor!" said a factory-girl.

Bee crimsoned.

"Stop laughing!" she said to me in a savage aside. "I wish I could stuff my handkerchief down his throat. Won't he ever stop?"

"It seems not!" I answered, cheerfully. "And we really can't consider that there is any more style to this manner of driving than if we belonged to the *hoi polloi* who drive with their husbands, and let their dogs follow, can we?"

Bee gave me a look.

"I believe you are pinching him to make him howl," she said.

At that unjust accusation I took my arms away from Jack's neck, and feeling the affectionate embrace of his lawful mistress relax, he violently eluded Bee's, and with a flying leap he was out and away, safely restored to his doggish dignity.

By this time quite a little crowd had collected, and Amos's shoulders were shaking unmistakably. Both these things annoyed Bee. The crowd was pitying her. Amos was laughing at her,—two things which could not fail to vex. She can bear being envied to the verge of being wished a violent death with equanimity, but to be pitied or ridiculed? Haughty Bee! She forgot herself, and gave the order herself to drive fast, and the way we drove back to Peach Orchard gave Jack something to do to keep up with us. We may have lacked the style of our driving out, but Bee said the pace was good for the sorrels. To me it savoured of the pace of fugitives from justice.

Lilian Bell

This episode, unfortunate as it had proved, would not have dampened Bee's ardour nor discouraged her in the least, had not Jack taken matters into his own paws. He seemed to connect Bee with his day of humiliation, and not only eyed her with deep aversion, but howled painfully whenever she cornered him. And as for the victoria—to this day, whenever it is taken out, Jack with one leap is under the barn by a private entrance which he tunnelled out for himself on that never-to-be-forgotten day when we endeavoured to introduce a London fashion by means of him.

Nevertheless, her other suggestions were carried out. The lovely wild tangle of berry-bushes and long grass was subdued. Our old-fashioned garden was hidden by a row of firs, while Bee set out beds of cannas and geraniums. To me it was simply hideous, but the look of complacency which Bee habitually wore as she thus brought us within the pale of civilization more than repaid me for any artistic losses we may have sustained. Bee was my sister and our guest, and could only be made happy by feeling that her coming had effected changes for the better and by being constantly entertained. What, then, was more simple than to content her with such entertainment as she had requested before she came, and by permitting her to smarten us up? To be sure, Aubrey used to tell me every night that he was going to dig up the bed of cannas and coleus the moment her back was turned, but as I, too, was quite willing to see that done, it seemed to me that I was treading a somewhat dangerous road with great discretion and a tact I never should get the credit for. Bee, I felt sure, regarded me as a fool for not having done all this at the beginning.

At Bee's request we joined the Country Club and the Copsely Golf Club, and I bought more clothes, and the Angel and I found ourselves in a set we never had cared for before, but which was amusing enough for a few weeks or months at most.

But the episode which broke the backbone of Bee's complacency and virtually gave us back our freedom was this:

True to her word, Bee got us an English coachman and a footman, and put them into a very smart and highly expensive livery. But the coachman only lasted a week, having too eagerly imbibed of the flowing bowl and being discovered by the Angel asleep in his new livery with his head sweetly pillowed on the recumbent body of the gentlest cow. This mortified Bee, for the men were, in a sense, her property, so she dismissed him, had his livery cleaned, and resolutely set herself to the somewhat difficult task of securing a coachman to fit the livery. I could, in this, give her no assistance, or, to speak more accurately, she would permit none, and finally she announced, with an air of triumph which plainly called for congratulations, that she had secured what she wanted.

The first time I saw my new coachman, there was something irritatingly familiar about him. He seemed to know me very well, too, and called me "Mis' Jardine" with a nod of the head as if we had formerly been pals. But under Bee's tutelage I was on terms of distant civility with my menials instead of knowing all their joys and sorrows as in the past.

But Bee was charmed with the *tout ensemble.* She said he matched the footman better than the Englishman did, because the Englishman was Irish anyway.

So that first afternoon Bee arranged to go to the Copsely Golf Club just at the close of the tournament, and to drive up when the porches would be filled with the players and their friends having tea. Bee likes to make a dramatic entrance, and often relates in tones of positive awe how she once saw a Frenchwoman in an opera-cloak composed entirely of white tulle run the whole length of the Grand Opera House in Paris in order to make the tulle, which was cut to resemble wings, float out diaphanously behind her.

So as we bowled smartly along, the sorrels having been reduced by hard driving until they were models of symmetry, the new victoria shining, our new liveries glittering in the eyes of the populace, and we ourselves ragged out, as Aubrey said, as if our motto had been, "Damn the expense," we certainly felt complacent.

"Now watch him pull the sorrels up," whispered Bee. "I taught him myself."

With that we arrived almost at a fire-engine pace in front of the club-house steps, and the carriage stopped. But to our horror, Bee's coachman leaned so far backward to pull up that his body was perfectly horizontal, and—yes—I was sure of it, he braced his foot against the dashboard to get a leverage. I have seen grocery-boys pull up and turn sidewise on their seats in exactly the same manner.

Bee's face was purple.

The sorrels, unaccustomed to such a jerk of their bits, instantly began to back, and two men rushed down the steps to our assistance. But Jehu was equal to the occasion. He slapped the horses' backs with the reins, and joyously drove our two off wheels up on to the lowest step of the club-house porch.

In that attitude we paused, and *I* got out. Bee, after an instant's hesitation, gracefully followed suit. Nor could you tell from her placid face that this was not always the way we made our approach.

As for me, I was in a spasm of laughter which Jehu saw.

"I'm sorry, Mis' Jardine," he said, as the gentlemen released the sorrels' heads, and he prepared to drive off the steps, "but these horses pulls more than Guffin's mare, and I can't get a purchase on 'em with this bad hand of mine."

Then I knew who he was! He drove Guffin's grocery wagon for two months, and had lost three fingers of his right hand!

Poor Bee! But she took it out on me on the way home for not having had presentable servants before she came.

Now that she has gone, Amos is driving the sorrels again, and they are getting fat.

# CHAPTER X

## OUR FIRST HOUSE-PARTY

It was Bee who suggested giving one, but then Bee thought up so many things for us to do while she was staying with us!

She invited her friends, Sir Wemyss and Lady Lombard, to spend a week at Peach Orchard, and when they accepted she said, to soothe my fright at being asked to entertain such grand personages, that if I would invite other people and make a house-party, it would take much of the responsibility off my shoulders, as then the guests would entertain each other.

Then she mentioned Mr. and Mrs. Jimmie, Artie Beguelin and his wife, Cary Farquhar, and Captain Featherstone, which would make ten of us in all.

To those who did not know Jimmie, this would seem a small number for a house-party, but Jimmie in a house all by himself would seem to fill it to overflowing with people, but they would all be Jimmie.

As I knew how much solid satisfaction it would be to Mrs. Jimmie to be for a whole week in the same house with so famous a beauty as Lady Lombard, I acted on Bee's suggestion, and all my people said they would come.

Bee came gracefully down-stairs one morning before our guests came. She held a letter in her hand.

"Coffee, Bee?" I asked.

"No, thank you. I had mine in bed."

She wrinkled her brow in perplexity.

"I don't know what to do about it," she murmured.

"About what?"

"Billy. He wants to see me so much, mother writes. She thinks I ought to come home immediately."

"Let's see," I said. "It's only eight months since you saw your child. Isn't mother rather absurd?"

Bee lifted her eyes.

"Don't be nasty," she said. "You learned that tone from Aubrey."

Aubrey smiled pleasantly at our guest.

"I didn't!" I said, warmly. "I used to be quite nasty at times before I was married."

Bee showed her little white teeth in a smile.

"I'm glad to hear you admit it," she said, sweetly.

"If you would like to see Billy so much," said Aubrey, politely, "why not bring him on here?"

"Could you?" I cried, in delight. To think of having Billy! The lamb had never been in the country in his life, and he was wild over my letters about Peach Orchard.

"I can arrange it, if you like," Aubrey went on—mostly to me, for Billy's mother was silently thinking.

"Do have him, Bee!" I cried. "I won't let him get in your way. He needn't even sleep in your room. I'll have Norah put up a cot in the alcove of the rose room. She can sleep there, and dress him and everything. You won't be annoyed the least bit."

"Well," said Bee, with graceful reluctance, "if you are sure he won't be in your way, and if Aubrey's cousin will bring him, I see no reason why he mightn't come."

I almost squealed in my delight. It would certainly be worth while to see the child's eyes when he first saw the calves and little chickens.

I left both Aubrey and Bee at the table while I rushed upstairs to see if the rose room would be just right for him. I made Aubrey promise to arrange everything by telegraph. Norah loved children, and entered into my plans with delight. Then I flew out to interview old Amos. He had told me only a few days before that the boys on the estate next ours wanted to sell their goats and goat carriages.

The days passed rapidly in preparations, but of all my guests, titled or otherwise, it was Billy—my Billy—I wanted to see worst. In two days I got a letter.

"Dear Miss Tats," it ran, "I only write to say that I shall be glad to come. If I had not written you a long letter so soon ago, I would write more now. Tell mother to be sure to meet me at the station. Don't let her forget that I shall arrive at four-sixteen. Your affectionate little nephew, Billy."

I wept tears of delight over this effusion, and "so soon ago" passed into the Jardine vocabulary.

In looking back, I think I can safely say that if Bee had known what would happen at that house-party to shock her English friends, she would have preferred to discharge her obligations to them by a nice little Sunday afternoon at Coney Island or an evening in Chinatown. But fortunately the English are a sensible race, and Sir Wemyss and his bride, perhaps because of the reasonable way the duchess came around when she found her daughter bent upon marrying Sir Wemyss, were so good-humoured and so plainly determined to see naught but good in America and naught but fun in Americans that they took everything in good part.

Aubrey, Jimmie, and Sir Wemyss got on capitally from the start, for before they came Aubrey said:

"What shall I say to them at first—when they come aboard of us, and before I have got my sea legs on?"

"Why," said Jimmie, "that's dead easy. Say to Lady Mary, 'Let my wife give you some tea,' and to Sir Wemyss say, 'Old man, how would a whiskey and soda go?' and there you are right off the bat."

Aubrey said precisely these words, with the most satisfactory result, for over her third cup of tea I felt very friendly with the beautiful English woman, and after four whiskies the men were almost sociable.

To our delight, Sir Wemyss was enchanted with Peach Orchard. He visited the uttermost corners of it. He was charmed with the cows, admired their breed, almost raved over Jack, the bulldog, whose pedigree was nearly as long as that of Lady Mary, who was the daughter of a hundred earls. He gave me many hints about my fine poultry, and wrote that first night for a pair of his very finest buff cochins to be sent over from his place in England, which he had just inherited from his uncle. He showed us where the apple-trees needed pruning, and was so interested in my attempts at an old-fashioned garden, which Bee had hidden behind a tall hedge, that he went to fetch Lady Mary to look at it, and they both volunteered to send me some plants and shrubs from England, which they declared I needed to complete it.

Bee's face was a study during those few hours. She had honestly tried to have everything as English as possible for them, and had trained my poor servants almost to death, with instructions as to what they were to do during this week. They were outwardly obedient, but inwardly disrespectful, as I overheard Norah, the housemaid, say to the cook:

"Katie, oh, Katie! We're wor-rkin' for the Four Hundhred now!"

"How do you know we ar-re?" asked Katie.

"The ladies all shtrip fur dinner!"

Jimmie simply shrieked when I told him, but Bee failed to see anything in it but an excellent reason why Norah should be discharged. Poor Bee!

She had given me specific directions about serving the

meals, and had made me lay in a supply of jam for breakfast, and had implored me to serve cold meats and joints and things as the English do, and to please her I had promised. But that first night at dinner Lady Mary turned to me and said, with a sweetness and grace not to be reproduced:

"Mrs. Jardine, I have come over here to live among you and to be as little unlike you Americans as possible. I cannot forget that it was the American dollar that made it possible for Wemyss to gain poor dear mamma's consent to our marriage, and I am correspondingly grateful. Now, won't you do me a favour? Won't you please leave off doing anything for us in the English manner, because of your desire to please us, and mayn't I see in your house just how Americans live. Particularly your breakfasts. I have heard that they were so jolly—not a bit like ours, and I am keen to taste your hot breads! Fancy! I never saw any in my life."

I fairly gasped with delight, and as for the maids, I was afraid they were going to kiss Lady Mary. It removed an awful strain.

"Certainly," I beamed. "I will do anything I can for you."

"If she does," declared Jimmie, "there won't be a queer American thing for you to learn after you leave Peach Orchard. You'll have seen 'em all."

"That is what I should like," said Lady Mary, in her deep, beautiful voice. "And Wemyss would, too."

Sir Wemyss, who spoke but seldom, here removed his cigar, for we had gone into the billiard-room after dinner, and said:

"Jardine, you don't know how a little place like this appeals to me. Now our places in England are all so large that they take an army of servants to run them, and the gardening and all that are done by one's men. But here with only yourselves you can do so much. You can feed your own chickens, you can prune your own trees, you can do such a lot yourselves. I should think it would be great fun."

We were much flattered by this view of it, and Mrs. Jimmie and Bee were plainly impressed.

"My sister is very fond of her life here," declared Bee. "I found Peach Orchard a perfect pastoral when I first came."

Jimmie had been smoking thoughtfully, with a frown of perplexity on his brow. Suddenly he spoke.

"I think Sir Wemyss is right," he answered. "Now, why not all of us take a hand at farming, so to speak, while we are here? I never have, but I know I could. Anyhow I mean to try. To-morrow, let's go at it and prune the trees."

"It is not the proper season to prune trees," observed Sir Wemyss. "That should be done in the early spring, before the sap begins to run."

Jimmie looked disappointed.

"Those apple-trees are no good," said the Angel, with tact, "so it couldn't possibly hurt to prune them or cut them down if you want to. They are a perfect eyesore to me the way they are."

To my surprise, both Jimmie and Sir Wemyss looked pleased. It was so palpably the wrong thing to do that I should have supposed as good a husbandman as Sir Wemyss would refuse. But the joy of doing evidently led him to accept the Angel's tactful permission to ruin our apple-trees, if by so doing he could interest our guests.

"The very thing!" said Sir Wemyss, with the nearest approach to enthusiasm I ever had seen in him. "Let's prune the trees by all means."

"How charming!" said Bee. "Isn't it delightful to be your own gardener! You have no idea how domestic my sister is, Lady Mary. She superintends her house quite like an English-woman. Did you know that we make all our own butter here at Peach Orchard, Sir Wemyss? And I verily believe that Faith knows every chicken on the place by name. She is really at her best on a farm."

Jimmie's cigar blinked as if he had winked with it. Mrs. Jimmie almost permitted herself a wry face at the idea of turning her one week with the Lombards to such poor account, and at first I feared that this plan would quite spoil her pleasure, to say nothing of Bee's. But if you have noticed, the hostess has very little to do with a modern house-party, except to get her people together. After that, they manage things to suit themselves.

At any rate, it occurred that way at my house-party. I had little to do except to trot uncomplainingly in the rear of the procession, for when once Lady Mary made farming fashionable by her personal interest, Bee, who always out-Herods Herod, became so bucolic that she nearly drove the hens off their nests in order to hatch the eggs personally.

On the second day from the date of his letter, Billy arrived. Bee and I went to meet him. The train did not stop at Clovertown, so we had to drive about ten miles. I shall never forget that child's face as he saw his mother. It twitched with feeling, but he felt himself too great a boy to cry—especially over joy. *I* cried heartily. I always do! And Billy comforted me in his sweet, babyish fashion that I remembered he used when he was in kilts.

Billy became friends with old Amos that first evening, and that sufficed, for Amos had enriched my own childhood, and I knew that nothing which could amuse or instruct would be omitted.

Billy felt that he and Jimmie, Aubrey, Captain Featherstone, and Sir Wemyss constituted the men of the household. When I asked him why he did not include Mr. Beguelin, he put his hands behind him, spread his short legs apart, and said:

"Well, you see, Miss Tats, Mr. Beguelin has just been married, and bridegrooms don't count."

Things went smoothly enough that first day while my people were becoming acquainted. Then it was Jimmie, dear blessed old, maladroit, hot-tempered Jimmie, always so completely at home in a business deal, and always so pathetically awkward and so confidently bungling in domestic crises, who supplied us with sufficient material for a book on "How Not to Prune Trees Properly."

We all went out to the apple-trees early in the morning. As usual, Sir Wemyss was dressed for the part. Why is it, I wonder, that the British always find themselves dressed for the occasion? I believe, if an Englishman were wrecked in mid-ocean, with only a hat-box for baggage, that out of that box he could produce bathing-trunks in which to drown properly.

The Angel was frankly and simply disreputable, his idea of being properly clad for farm-work being to be ragged wherever possible and faded all over. Jimmie, however, wore his ordinary business clothes, patent leather shoes, and a derby hat. And as events transpired, I was glad of it. I love to think of Jimmie pruning trees in patent leathers and a derby.

Being, as I say, confident, Jimmie, who never had seen a tree pruned, waited for no instructions, but sprang nimbly upon a barrel, and, standing on his tiptoes, reached up and snipped at the lower branches. Sir Wemyss took a ladder and his pruning-knife, and disappeared from view into the thickest part of the tree. But hearing the industry of Jimmie's scissors, he parted the branches and called out:

"I say there, old man! You are cutting off twigs. These are the things which need to go—these suckers. See?"

"Yes, Jimmie," I said, pleasantly. "You are not trimming a hedge, you know. You are—"

Alas, that accidents are always my fault! Jimmie turned to glare at me, and the treacherous barrel-head gave way, letting him down most ungently into its middle, and rasping his shins in the descent in a manner which must have been particularly trying to one of delicate sensibilities.

I sank down suddenly in gasps of unregenerate laughter, for the barrel-head was a tight fit, and as Jimmie endeavoured to climb out, the barrel climbed too, giving him a strange hoop-skirt effect, which went but sadly with the derby hat.

Jimmie grinned sheepishly as the Angel extricated him, and placed a strong board on the barrel for him to stand upon in safety.

Then Jimmie decided to saw a dead limb off, and leave the pruning to Sir Wemyss. So he took the saw and went valiantly to work, but it was tiresome, so he leaned his weight against the limb and industriously sawed his prop off, which sent him flying almost into Lady Mary's lap. He saved himself by his nimbleness, but this time Jimmie was mad— uncompromisingly mad.

He said little, however, but seated himself in the cooling and tranquil vicinity of his Madonna-faced wife, while watching the Angel and Sir Wemyss reduce the refractory tree to symmetry and healthfulness without effort and without disaster.

His failure and particularly Bee's and my ghoulish laughter had nettled him, however, and he was determined to recover himself as well as regain his place in our esteem.

All day he wandered around, seeking a suitable opportunity, all the while watching me craftily to see if I suspected his design. But I gave no sign, which plainly lightened the burden he was carrying.

Lady Mary trained my crimson rambler rose over the dining-room window and cut flowers for all the vases. This was ordinarily my work, and I loved it, but it gave her pleasure, and above all it gave her a home pleasure which she had missed. I asked her if she would train the roses every day while she was with us, taking the work off my hands. She coloured softly as she gladly consented, and went prettily and importantly to work.

Artie Beg, having just come home from a prolonged honey-moon, was frequently obliged to go into town for a few hours' conference with his partner, and Cary, from being one of the most energetic of guests, had developed a tendency to talk of nothing in the world except her husband, and, when no one would listen to her, of sitting apart with her hands folded in her lap and a dreamy look in her eyes as if only her body were present at my house-party. Her mind was plainly in Wall Street.

I may not be believed, but Christianity and the love of God were working in my heart when the next afternoon I asked Jimmie's help in a piece of work which it did not seem possible for him to fail in.

The side porch has a great curving, bulging iron trellis for the honeysuckle, and I keep the vines so thinned out that I can have boxes of flowers growing on the porch railing, which only need what sunlight comes filtering through the honeysuckle. By cutting the blossoms every day I obtain the result I wish, and on this occasion I had cut all I could reach, and I asked Jimmie to cut those which were beyond me.

These boxes at the bottom were only as wide as the porch railing, but flared out on both sides in order to hold more earth, and all were painted green. Now in that particular box, shaded by the honeysuckle, I had, with infinite care, coaxed sun-loving dwarf nasturtiums to grow, because their gorgeous colouring looked so well next to the box which held my ferns.

I had planted the nasturtiums in early spring in the box in the greenhouse, shading the colours from pale yellow at each end to a glorious orange and crimson in the middle. Each plant was perfect of its kind and growing and blooming riotously before I took the box, which was some fourteen feet long, and with my own hands nailed it to the porch railing, and its ends to two pillars.

It never occurred to me that Jimmie would be foolish enough to try to *stand* on the edge of that box, for of course, while I am no carpenter, I drove my nails to cope with wind-storms, not a great man, who—oh, well! I might have known that Jimmie would do something.

He could have reached all I wanted from the porch, but of course, though I only stepped through the French window to lay my flowers down, in that instant Jimmie had sprung upon that slanting edge of my poor, frail little box, and in that instant the mischief was done. The box tilted and flung Jimmie forward against the curving trellis, which began to creak and groan alarmingly. All my precious nasturtiums were pitched headlong into the flower-beds below, and for once Jimmie shrieked my name in accents of the acutest entreaty.

"Faith!" he shouted, below his breath. "Faith, for God's sake run here and catch me! This damned thing is giving way. Haul me back. Oh, my coat won't save me! Leggo my coat-tails. Put your arms around my waist. Stop laughing! Put—your—arms—around my waist—I say—and haul me back! Brace your feet and pull!"

I did as he desired, bracing my feet and dragging him back to safety by his leather belt.

We were detected, however, by Bee and Captain Feather-stone, who came strolling gracefully around the corner of the house just as Jimmie's convulsed clutch loosened from the trellis and set all the vines to dancing and trembling, as if a wind-storm had passed over them.

There was no need of their asking what had happened. The ruin spoke for itself. Captain Featherstone gallantly helped me to pick up and replant my poor nasturtiums, but they had been so bruised and their feelings so wounded by their undignified tumble that they did nothing but sulk all the remainder of the summer, never once blooming out handsomely as they should, although I carefully explained to them just how it happened. They seemed to think that it was my fault, and they never forgave me. Sometimes flowers are as unreasonable as people.

Three days after Billy's arrival, when he had thoroughly mastered all the details of Peach Orchard and knew personally all the cows, the horses, the white bulldog, the cats, the chickens, the little calves, and the reachable branches of every tree on the place, old Amos came in to speak to me.

He stood before me, bowing, with his hat in his hand:

"Well'm, Miss Faith honey, I reckon de time's about ripe foh de goats. Dat boy's investigated every nook an' cornder ob de place, an' ef you tink bes' I'll go after de goats dis afternoon."

"Very well, Amos," I said. "We are all going to Philadelphia to-day to attend the launching of Mr. Beguelin's yacht, and we are going to take Billy. You can bring the goats up while we are away, and tomorrow morning we can give them to him."

"Yas'm," said Amos, bowing. "I'll have 'em hyah when y'all gets back."

I will say nothing of the ceremony of the launching of the yacht, although, from Cary's uplifted face, you would have thought it was the christening of a first-born child. Jimmie says we needn't say anything. We were worse!

Billy was wildly excited over the breaking of the bottle of champagne, and asked a thousand questions about it.

The next morning we all went out to the barn to see him receive his goats. His face fairly beamed when he saw them. He clapped his hands.

"Oh, Uncle Aubrey! Miss Tats! Are they for me?"

Then he flung his arms around his mother's neck—Bee's neck, mind you!—and cried out:

"Oh, mother, I do think I have the kindest relatives in all the world! What other little boys' relatives would think of the kindness of giving them goats?"

"That's right, my boy," said Captain Featherstone, looking with open admiration at Bee's motherly attitude, on her knees beside her boy and his arms around her neck, "always be grateful. It's a rare virtue these days."

Jimmie, however, who always spoils things, winked at Aubrey. But Billy's next remark threw us all into fits of laughter.

"Oh, Uncle Aubrey, can't we have a ceremony of launching the goats, and mayn't I break a bottle of champagne over their horns?"

Jimmie fairly yelled. Billy looked distressed.

"Their horns are very strong!" he urged. "I don't believe it would hurt them one bit. And you might give me one of those little bottles I saw Mr. Jimmie open—you remember the little one you had after the two big ones, don't you, Mr. Jimmie?"

"Oh, yes, Billy," I said. "Mr. Jimmie remembers. (You'd be ashamed not to, wouldn't you, Jimmie?)"

"You think you're funny," growled Jimmie, witheringly, as Sir Wemyss and Captain Featherstone broke out afresh, and even Artie Beg left off looking at Cary long enough to smile at Jimmie's scarlet face and Mrs. Jimmie's anxious one. She moved quietly over to where Jimmie was standing with his hands in his pockets, and slipped her arm through his. She did not know quite what it was all about, but she felt that they were laughing at her Jimmie, and, as usual, she looked reproachfully at me.

Billy's plaintive voice recalled us.

"Yes, dearie," I hastened to say. "You may have a small bottle of champagne—or perhaps Apollinaris water would be better, it sparkles just the same, and if it flew in the goats' eyes it wouldn't make them smart, and the champagne would."

Billy beamingly acquiesced.

"Now I must just think up some good names for them," he said, with an air of importance, "and perhaps I'll have to ask Uncle Aubrey and Mr. Jimmie to help me. It's awful hard to think up suitable names for goats."

"All right, old man," said Aubrey. "Come along. We'll think 'em up now, and have the launching this afternoon, and invite some people to the ceremony."

So he and Billy and Jimmie took leave of us, and strolled away together, Billy with his hands in his trousers' pockets and striving to take just as long steps as they did. He would have given his kingdom for a pipe!

We got up quite a little party, and worked very hard over it. Bee and Captain Featherstone delivered the invitations, and people thought it was a most delicious joke, and came in a mood of the utmost hilarity. At first Billy wanted to break the bottle himself, but upon being told that girls always did it, he invited a bewitching little maid of seven, Kathleen Van Osdel, to christen them, while Billy valiantly sat in the goat-carriage, waiting for Aubrey and Amos to let go of the goats' horns.

The names were kept a profound secret, but Jimmie had a fashion of going purple in the face, and pretending he was only going to sneeze. He walked around among the guests trying to appear unconcerned—which made me watch him closely.

He had appointed himself master of ceremonies. He it was who put the Apollinaris bottle into Kathleen's hands, and held her in his arms while she leaned down and broke the bottle over the horns of the gentler goat.

Then her childish treble shrilled out:

"I christen thee, Roosevelt and Congress!" she cried out.

"Let go!" shouted Billy, standing up in the goat carriage, his cheeks like scarlet flowers.

Amos and Aubrey released their hold, Kathleen screamed with excitement, and away bounded the goats down the driveway, with Sir Wemyss after them on horseback, for fear anything might happen.

But nothing did happen, and in ten minutes back they came to receive congratulations from everybody.

"Are they all right, Billy?" I cried.

"Yes, Miss Tats. Congress is just as gentle as can be when you let him alone. They go splendidly, except when Roosevelt butts. You know he is always butting into Congress and making trouble."

At that I understood, for Jimmie deliberately rolled on the grass.

"I noticed that peculiarity of the goats," he gasped, when he could speak, "but if I had trained that child a month, he couldn't have put it better. It's—it's simply too good to be true!"

Then he went away to explain the joke to Lady Mary.

I think Bee enjoyed the house-party in spite of its gardening flavour, for we entertained quite a little. At another time I gave a musicale, and had people out from town; we were invited about while automobiles snorted and chunked into Peach Orchard at all hours of the day to the everlasting terror of the cats, who streaked by us and flashed up trees in simple lines of long gray fur.

It was strange how the cat family resembled human beings, for it was the young cats, Puffy and Pinkie and Fitz and Corbett, who got used to the automobiles first, and ceased to run at their approach. Youth is ever progressive and adaptable, while poor old Mitnick crouched in the fork of a high pine, and glared with her yellow eyes and waved her great tail in furious revolt at those puffing, snorting monsters which she never could abide anyway,—and she was glad she couldn't.

We had no automobile, but the sorrels were there in the height of their glory and slimness, and we still basked in the refulgence of the coachman and footman of Bee's own selection, so her soul was at peace.

Only one thing happened to mar our pleasure. Jimmie fell ill.

Mrs. Jimmie hunted me up one blistering morning, and said, anxiously:

"Faith, I am very much worried about Jimmie. He is lying down."

"Well, what of it?" I said, with unintentioned brutality. "Does he always sit up that you seem so surprised?"

She looked at me reproachfully.

"He always sits up when he is well," she said, gently.

"Is he ill?" I exclaimed, dropping my gardening shears and hastily wiping my hands on my apron. "Can I do anything for him? Does he need a doctor? I'll go right up."

Mrs. Jimmie coloured all over her soft creamy face. She laid her hand on my arm.

"Don't be offended, will you, dear?" she begged, "but—Jimmie—you know how unreasonable sick men are—"

She paused helplessly.

I waited.

"Well, out with it! What does he want?"

"He said—I didn't realize how difficult it would be to tell you when he said it—but he said—"

Again she stopped.

"I shall evidently have to go and ask him what he wants," I said, moving toward the house.

"No, no, dear! I will tell you! Don't go near him!" pleaded Mrs. Jimmie. "That is just what he doesn't want. He said on no account were you to come near him."

She paused with a gasp. Evidently she expected me to burst into tears.

"The brute!" I remarked, pleasantly. "I hope he is suffering!"

Mrs. Jimmie's beautiful face became instantly grave.

"He is suffering, Faith," she said, quietly.

"Then why won't he see me? Perhaps I could do something. Aubrey always lets me try. Has he a headache?"

"He has a splitting headache, he says, and a high fever, and his collar hurts him."

"His collar hurts him! Then why doesn't he take it off?"

"That's just it. He won't. He says he always wears it and it never hurt him before, and he'll be—well, he says he won't take it off for anybody."

I turned away and bit my lip.

Poor old sick, obstinate Jimmie! In my mind's eye I could just see him lying there with all his hot clothes on and swearing he would not take them off and be made comfortable.

But I could do nothing. He would see none of us. I sent tea and lemonade and ice and hot-water bags and every conceivable remedy to his rooms, but with no effect. Nor would he hear of our calling a doctor.

About four o'clock Mrs. Jimmie left him for a few moments, and this was my chance.

I slipped into the room. He was lying on the couch with his feet in patent leather shoes,—even his coat and waistcoat on, and a high, tight collar which rasped his ears.

He grinned sheepishly when he saw me.

"You told me to keep out, I know, but I never do as I'm told, so I came anyhow."

"I know that," growled Jimmie.

"Your head's as hot as fire," I said. "And those shoes are drawing like a mustard plaster."

"I don't care. I won't take 'em off," said Jimmie, savagely, raising himself on his elbow.

I turned on him.

"You always were a fool, Jimmie," I said. "You don't have to take them off if you don't want to." (He sank back with a groan of pain.) "But I'm going to do it, and if you kick while your foot is in my lap you'll hurt me."

Before he could wink I had pulled off those abominable things, and slipped his narrow silk-stockinged feet into cool slippers. He couldn't restrain a sigh of comfort. I went in the closet to put his shoes on their trees, and brought out a white linen coat.

"Sit up and put this on," I commanded.

"I will not!" he answered, flatly.

I looked around and there stood Mrs. Jimmie. If she had stayed away another ten minutes, I would have got him comfortable. But in spite of our combined efforts he insisted upon lying there as he was.

I went out and telephoned for the doctor, and when he came it pleased Jimmie no end that he didn't say a word about taking off those hot clothes.

"You see," he said to his wife, "that doctor knows his business. He doesn't devil me the way you women do."

Mrs. Jimmie was wise enough to make no reply.

"He said if you would go to sleep for an hour you would feel better," she said. "So put on this thin coat, then I'll close the blinds and go out."

Jimmie looked at her quizzically. Then he slowly sat up and changed his coat without a word.

When he wakened his headache was gone. But he was unable to come down to dinner, and we saw him no more that day.

As he went to bed that night he said:

"I suppose you and Faith chuckled over getting your own way with my shoes and coat. But I want you to tell Faith that I stuck it out on the collar and that I only took it off when I went to bed!"

He was all right the next day, so we were spared the grief of being obliged to bury him in that collar.

So it came to be the last day of the Lombards' stay.

We had all grown exceedingly fond of the dear English people who had come so sweetly into the midst of an American home and adapted themselves to our way of living with such easy grace. No one would have believed, to see Lady Mary in her simple garden hat and cotton gown, that she was a court beauty, over whose hand royalty had often bent in gracious admiration. But it was true.

Nor was she deficient in a sense of humour, for she openly doted on Jimmie, and listened intently for his jokes, with the laudable intention of seeing them before they were explained to her, if she could.

His absurd misadventures, however, came well within her ken, and this last one so tickled her fancy that—I blush to say it, but it is true—our imported Guernsey cow is responsible for Jimmie's invitation to Combe Abbey to visit the Duchess of Strowther, when Lady Mary goes home to her mother next May.

This is how it happened.

We were all out on the tennis-court one afternoon, when our attention was attracted by the strange antics of the Guernsey. She was generally quite shy and would allow no one to whom she was not accustomed to come near her. But on this occasion she lurched up near where we were standing, and crossed her forefeet and leered at us in such a way that we women instinctively moved backward and put the men between us and her.

We all stared at her, and she stared back and switched her long tail and hung her tongue out and rolled from side to side, until Jimmie said:

"I'm blessed if the old girl doesn't look drunk!"

Just then old Amos ambled up, his fat sides shaking.

"Dat's jest what!" he exclaimed. "You sho'ly am a jedge ob jags, Mistah Jimmie, tah be able tah tell 'em in man er beas'! Dat cow's drunk. Dat's what she is. Jest plain drunk an' disorderly. She broke her rope dis mornin' en got at de apples en filled hersif full ob dem. And apples always mek a cow drunk!"

"I never heard of such a thing," said Captain Featherstone.

Amos scratched his head.

"Well, Mars Captain, I reckon dere's a heap o' tings about a farm dat army ossifers never hearn tell of—meaning no onrespect to dere book larnin'. But jes' de same, dat air Guernsey am drunk."

We all looked at her with interest.

"But what will she do?" I said. "How does being drunk affect a cow?"

"Jes' same as er man, Miss Faith, honey. Jes' look at her! She used to be de shyest, mos' ladylake cow awn de place. She always seemed to 'member dat she'd had a calf en was a lady ob quality. Now look at her! She don' keer! She'd jes' as soon lean her head on de Boss's shoulder en ax him fer a drink er de loan ob his cee-gyar. She's done forgot dat she's a mudder. She feels lake she don' know which is de odder side ob de street en she don' want to be tol'! Dat's what drink does for man or beas'."

"But will it hurt her milk?" I said, soberly, for the rest were screaming at the imbecile expression of the Guernsey while Amos thus diagnosed her case.

"No'm, no'm. Leastways hit won't hurt huh none. It'll dry her up, dough. Such a jag as dat Guernsey's got will dry up her milk for two weeks er mo'. En I wouldn't keer to be de one ter milk huh, neider!"

Here was Jimmie's opportunity.

"Nonsense!" he said. "I'll milk her! I'm not afraid of what a drunken cow will do. Let me know, Amos, when you want her milked."

"All right, Mistah Jimmie. I sho will let you know, yas, sir. Now den, Missus fool cow! Ef you can leab off chattin' wid de quality long enough to go teh yo' stall, I'll show you de way."

I repeat—the Guernsey used to be our best-behaved, most intelligent and ladylike cow, but when Amos endeavoured to lead her away, she calmly sank down just where she was, and went to sleep.

This was too much for Amos. Fun was fun, to be sure, and he seemed glad we were pleased by the Guernsey's antics, but his wrath at a cow's taking the tennis-court for her afternoon nap upset his ideas of propriety.

"Doesn't she remind you for all the world," cried Jimmie, with tears in his eyes, "of a man who sinks to sleep with his arm affectionately around a lamp-post? Her feet are in an attitude that a painter would call 'one of unstudied grace!'"

But Amos, in a fury, pushed, pulled, slapped, and shoved her into a sitting posture, and, by dint of leaning upon each other as if both were under the weather, he finally got her started toward the barn, she, every once in awhile, pausing to lift a fore foot hilariously before planting it on her next uncertain step.

Several hours later I saw Jimmie, with a shining new milk-pail on his arm, followed by Amos with the milking-stool in his hand and his tongue in his cheek, go toward the Guernsey's stall.

We all looked expectantly at each other, then rose, as if by common consent, and followed.

Lady Mary tucked her arm under Mrs. Jimmie's, and gurgled deliciously.

"Oh, dear Mrs. Jimmie! Is your husband always as amusing as he has been here at Peach Orchard? If he is, I am sure mamma would just delight in him—only things aren't always happening at Combe Abbey to show him off as they are at Mrs. Jardine's."

Mrs. Jimmie looked dubious at the first part of this remark, flushed with pleasure at the middle of it, and looked reproachfully at me at the last.

Why is everything always my fault, I wonder?

"Well, I don't know," she said, slowly, "but it does seem as if Jimmie always gets into more troub—I mean, has more adventures when he and Faith are together than when he and I are alone. Oh, oh! What can be the matter with that cow! Oh, I wonder if she has killed my husband!"

We all looked just in time to see the Guernsey gallop madly across the garden, plough her way through the sweet corn, and disappear gaily over the fence, heading for the trolley-tracks, with Amos a close second as she took the hurdle.

Bee's English coachman, who took great pride in the kitchen-garden, hastily followed to see what damage she had done, but at Mrs. Jimmie's agonized entreaty to know what had become of Jimmie, I called him, and he came, respectfully touching his forelock in a way which Jimmie always said "was worth the price of admission."

"I think she has about done for the Country Gentleman, ma'am. She has trampled it so it will never be any good."

Mrs. Jimmie turned white, and leaned gaspingly on Lady Mary.

"Trampled him!" she cried. "Oh, come! Come quickly, and see if she has killed him!"

"My dear!" I cried, almost hysterical over her mistake. "The Country Gentleman is a kind of sweet corn—not Jimmie! See, there he is now. Look, dearest!"

Sure enough, there came Jimmie, a trifle sheepish, but defiant. His derby hat was without a brim, the milk-pail was jammed together like a folding lunch-box, and had a little foam on the outside, as the sole product of his milking prowess.

We asked no questions, but our eager faces demanded an explanation.

He gave it,—terse as was his wont.

"Well, I'll bet that damned cow never switches her tail in anybody's face again!"

We needed no further description of what had happened. The picture was complete.

Strange to say, Lady Mary seemed to comprehend better than any of us. She gurgled with laughter the whole evening, and lavished attentions upon Jimmie so flatteringly that he ceased to look furtively at me and became quite cocky before the evening was over, pretending that he had done all these things to help me entertain my guests.

As we went up-stairs that night, Mrs. Jimmie clutched my arm, and, with eyes as big as stars, said, in a tense whisper:

"My dear, we are invited to Combe Abbey! Think of it! To visit the Duchess of Strowther! Lady Mary is going to write to her mother immediately!"

If it had been anybody except dear Mrs. Jimmie, I should have said:

"Is she going to invite the cow, too?"

But as it was, I squeezed back, and said, earnestly:

"I am so glad, dear Mrs. Jimmie!"

# CHAPTER XI

## ON THE GENTLE ART OF
## WASTING OTHER PEOPLE'S TIME

On the last day of the house-party we decided to hold a family gathering in the evening, to which each guest must bring a written sketch of some member of the household. It was to be a very short sketch, not to consume over ten minutes in the reading, and no one was to get angry, and no one was to get his feelings hurt.

Aubrey had to go into New York to attend a dress rehearsal of his new play, but he promised to write something on the train, and have it ready. His absence left me at once to play hostess and to receive the queer, curious, and inconsequent persons who flock to the door of the successful playwright, with every wish from obtaining his autograph to an offer to stage his plays.

My time was all taken up until eleven o'clock, in ordering and setting the servants at work, righting their wrongs, and pottering around among my large family. At three I had an engagement. This left me but a short time in which to write my sketch. I begged Bee to help me out, but never yet have I succeeded in impressing Bee with any respect for my working hours. For this reason I laid down the law with open energy to Billy, hoping that Bee would see that I meant her.

I began the campaign at breakfast. Bee and Billy and I were alone.

"At eleven o'clock I am going to begin to write," I announced, firmly, "and, Billy, I want you distinctly to understand that you are not to run your engine in my hall. Do you hear?"

"Um—huh," said Billy, smiling at me like a cherub.

Bee leaned over and wiped the butter off Billy's chin.

"Before I go to town to-day I want to talk over that blue silk with you," she said. "I don't know how much to get, and Eugenie is so extravagant unless I get the stuff and tell her I got all there was in the piece. Then she makes it do. Would you have it made up with lace?"

"Now, look here, Bee," I said, "I am not going to get my head all muddled with dressmaking before I begin to write. I have all my ideas ready to write that article for to-night. I am going to tell about Mr. and Mrs. Jimmie at Canterbury. Don't you remember what happened? You know if you side-track me on clothes I simply cannot do a thing."

"I know," said Bee, placidly. "No, Billy, not another lump of sugar. Be quiet while mamma talks to Tattah. I know, but it seems to me you might have selected another day to write. You know I wanted to consult you about the dinner Thursday."

"I didn't select the day. The day selected me."

"Why didn't you write yesterday?"

"I didn't have any time."

"Why don't you wait until afternoon?"

"You know they are to be read tonight."

"Oh, very well, go ahead, and I won't bother you. I dare say the dinner will be all right. But if you would just tell me which to use, lace or chiffon with the blue?"

"Lace," I said, in desperation.

Bee half-way closed her eyes and took Billy's hand out of the cream-pitcher.

"I think I'll use chiffon," she said.

The only use my advice is to Bee is to fasten her on to the opposite thing. She says I help her to decide because I am always wrong.

"Now will you keep Billy away and excuse me to all visitors, and don't come near my door for three hours and send my luncheon up at one o'clock, and *don't send after the tray*! Leave it there until I have finished writing."

"It is so untidy," murmured Bee.

"Well, who will see it?"

I am one of those who cleanse the outside of the desk and the bureau.

"Now, Billy, my precious, if you will keep away from Tattah all the morning, I will give you some candy directly after dinner. You will find it on the sconce just where I always put it," I said.

The sconce is where Billy and I put things for each other. He is only three and a half—"thrippence, ha'penny," he says if you ask him, but beguiling—oh, as beguiling as Cleopatra, or the serpent in the Garden of Eden, or—or as his mother!

Billy and I went to look at the sconce on my way up-stairs, and he called me back twice, saying, "Tattah, I want to kiss you," which I could but feel was something due to the promised candy on the sconce.

I sat down and began to write:

*Mr. and Mrs. Jimmie at Canterbury.*

Mrs. Jimmie, having been presented at the Court of St. James, always has more to do in London than she can attend to. As Jimmie hates functions with all the hatred of the American business man who looks upon gloves as for warmth only, this leaves Jimmie and me to roam around London at will. Mrs. Jimmie loathes the top of a "'bus" and absolutely draws the line at "The Cheshire Cheese." She lunches at Scott's and dines at the Savoy, while Jimmie and I are never so happy as in the grill-room at the Trocadero or in a hansom, threading the mazes of the City, bound for a plate of beefsteak pie at "The Cheshire Cheese" or on top of a 'bus on Saturday night, going through the Whitechapel region, creepy with horrors of "Jack the Ripper."

"What in all the world is a beefsteak pie?" she asked us, when she heard our unctuous exclamations.

"Why, it is a huge meat pie, made out of ham and larks and pigeons and beef, with a delicious gravy or sauce and a divine pastry. And you eat it in a little old kitchen with a sanded floor and deal tables, and where the bread is cut in chunks and where the steins are so thick that it is like drinking your beer over a stone wall, and where Dr. Samuel Johnson used to sit so often that the oil from his hair has made a lovely dirty spot on the wall, and they have it under glass with a tablet to his memory, so that if you like you can go and kneel down and worship before it, with your knees grinding into the sand of the floor," I said.

"Dear me," said Mrs. Jimmie, faintly. "Couldn't they have cleaned it off?"

At this juncture Bee came in with her hat on. "Excuse me for interrupting you," she said, with a far-away look in her eyes. "But do you mind if I copy that pink negligee? It hangs so much better than those I got in Paris. I won't take a moment. Just stand up and let me see. You needn't look so despairing, I am not going to stay. No, Billy, you stay there. Mother will be down directly. Oh, baby, why will you step on poor Tattah's gown? See, you hurt her. Didn't I tell you to stay with Norah? Six, eight, ten   don't, Billy. Don't touch any of Tattah's papers. Twelve—and four times seven—I think thirty yards of lace—Billy, take your engine off the piano. Oh, I forgot to tell you that Dick just telephoned, and wants us to make up a party for the theatre, with a supper afterward, next Monday. I telephoned to Freddie and asked him, and he is delighted, and so I told Dick that we would all come with pleasure. Now come, Billy, we must not interrupt Tattah. This is one of the days when she must not be disturbed."

She closed the door with the softness one uses in closing the door of a death-chamber, in order, I suppose, "not to disturb" me. I pulled myself together, and went on.

*Mr. and Mrs. Jimmie at Canterbury.*

"Clean it off? What sacrilege! Why, there are persons who would like to buy the whole wall, as Taffy tried to buy the wall on which Little Billee had drawn Trilby's foot," I exclaimed.

Mrs. Jimmie looked incredulous. She is so deliciously lacking in a sense of humour that in the frivolous society of Jimmie and me she is as much out of place as the Venus de Milo would be in vaudeville.

"We had such a delightful day at Stoke Pogis Monday, how would you like to spend Sunday at Canterbury?" she said. "It seems to me that it would be a most restful thing to wander through that lovely old cathedral on Sunday."

Before I could reply, Jimmie dug his hands down in his pockets, thrust his legs out in front of him, dropped his chin on his shirt-bosom and chuckled.

"What I like are cheerful excursions," he said. "On Monday we went to Stoke Pogis. It rained, and we had to wear overshoes, and we carried umbrellas. We lunched at a nasty little inn where we had to eat cold ham and cold mutton and cold beef, when we were wet and frozen to start with. What I wanted was a hot Scotch and a hot chop and hot potatoes—everything *hot*. Then—"

"Wait," I cried. "It was the inn where John Storm and Glory Quayle lunched that day when she led him such a dance."

"John Fiddlesticks!" said Jimmie. "As if that counted against that cold lunch! Then we arranged to go in the wagonette, but you got into such a hot argument with me—"

"I thought you said we didn't have anything hot," I murmured.

"Then we missed the wagonette, and spent an hour finding a cab. Then when we got there we were waylaid by an old woman in a little cottage, who showed us a register of tourists, and who artfully mentioned the sums they had given toward the restoration of Stoke Pogis, and you made me give more than the day's excursion cost. Then we went along a wet, bushy lane that muddied my trousers, and when we arrived at Gray's grave, you found the solemn yew-tree, and perched yourself on a wet, cold gravestone, and read Gray's Elegy aloud, while I held an umbrella over your heads and enjoyed myself. Now you want to put in Sunday at Canterbury, where, if it isn't more cheerful, you will probably have to bury me."

"Jimmie, you haven't any soul!" I said, in disgust.

Jimmie grunted.

A knock on the door.

"Please excuse me for interrupting you," said Mary, "but there are two reporters down-stairs, who want to know if they may photograph the front of the house for the Sunday *Battle Ax*."

"Yes, I don't care. Tell them to go ahead."

She shut the door and went away.

*Mr. and Mrs. Jimmie at Canterbury.*

"Oh, Jimmie," sighed his wife.

Another knock.

"Mary, what *do* you want?" I said, savagely.

She stuttered.

"And please, Missis, they want to know if you will just come and sit on the doorstep a moment with a book in your hand. I told them Mr. Jardine wasn't at home, so they said you would do!"

"No, I won't. Tell my sister to put on my hat and hold the book in front of her face and be photographed for me."

"Very well, Missis."

She went out, and again I numbered the page and essayed to write. But I could not. I was rapidly becoming mired. I stonily refused to leave my desk, but sat staring at the wall, trying to get the thread of my narrative, when—Mary again.

She was in tears.

"I am afraid to speak to you, and I am afraid *not* to speak to you," she stammered.

"Well, what is it?"

"Indeed, I try, Missis, but I can't seem to help you any. There are two young girls in the drawing-room, who want to know if Mr. Jardine will give his autograph to the Highland Alumnae Club. It has 472 members. They sent up their cards."

I simply moaned.

"That will be a whole hour's work! I can't do it now. (Mary knows I always write Aubrey's autographs for him!) Tell them to leave the cards and call for them to-morrow."

*Mr. and Mrs. Jimmie at Canterbury.*

"How in the world, Mrs. Jimmie, did you come to throw yourself away on Jimmie?" I said, with an impertinence which was only appreciated by Jimmie.

Mrs. Jimmie took me with infinite seriousness, and looked horrified at the sacrilege. She got up and crossed the room and sat down beside Jimmie on the sofa, without saying a word. Her tall, full figure towered above the gentlemanly slouch of Jimmie's boyish proportions, and her thus silently arraying herself on Jimmie's side as a wordless rebuke to my impertinence was so delicious that Jimmie gave me a solemn wink, as he said:

"Now she has only voiced the opinion of the world. Let us face the question once for all. Why did you marry me?"

Mrs. Jimmie coloured all over her creamy pale face. She looked in distress from me to Jimmie, divided between her desire to express in one burst of eloquence the fulness of her reasons for marrying the man she adored, and her reluctance to display emotion before me. She took everything with such edifying gravity. It never dawned on her that he was teasing her.

"Don't torment her so!" I said. "Mrs. Jimmie, I admire your taste, but I admire Jimmie's more."

"Thank you, dear," she said, seriously, but still with that soft blush on her cheeks. Then she added, quietly, "Jimmie never torments me."

"*Mon Dieu*," I said, under my breath, with a fierce glance at Jimmie. But he only shook his head, as one would who had not "fetched it" that time, but who meant to keep on trying.

Another knock. Mary again, with the mail. She was swallowing violently, and her eyes were full of tears. I took up the letters and tore them open.

Sixteen requests for autographs, only one enclosing a stamp. Twelve letters from young girls, telling Aubrey their stellar capabilities. Four requests for photographs. Some personal letters, and this choice effusion, which I copy *verbatim et spellatim.*

"DEAR SIR: Please tell me how you Study human natur do you travle extensively through close Social relations or do you Study phenology. You illustrate it So accrately that I would be pleased to know your method and if you don't think I am too cheeky, would be pleased to know your income. I remain yours with respect."

I gave a little shriek of delight, and rushed back to the Jimmies with renewed enthusiasm. This unknown man had inspired me afresh.

*Mr. and Mrs. Jimmie at Canterbury.*

But although Jimmie growls, there is no one in the world who is so excellent a travelling companion as he, for he is always ready for everything. You cannot suggest any jaunt too wild or too impossible for Jimmie not to bend his energies toward making it possible. The chief reason that Mrs. Jimmie likes me so much is because I admire Jimmie, and the reason that Jimmie likes me is because I adore Mrs. Jimmie.

So I was not at all surprised to find ourselves at Canterbury on Saturday afternoon, after a short run from London through one of the loveliest counties of England. Such bewitching shades of green. Such lovely little hills,—

friendly, companionable little hills. I can't bear mountains. It is like trying to be intimate with queens and empresses. They overpower me.

Canterbury was enchanted ground to me. We found the very old cellar over which stood the Canterbury Inn. I could picture the whole thing to myself. I even reconciled Chaucer's spelling with the quaintness and curiousness of the old, old town.

We strolled up to St. Martin's Church, said to be the oldest church in England, and wandered around the churchyard, filled with glorious roses creeping everywhere over tombs so old that the lettering is illegible. When the sun set, we had the most beautiful view of Canterbury to be had anywhere, and one of the most beautiful in all England.

We sat down to a cold supper that night in a charming little inn with diamond-paned windows. But as Jimmie loves Paris cooking and would almost barter his chances of heaven for a smoking dish of *sole a la Normande* at the Cafe Marguery, he cast looks of deep aversion at a side table loaded with all sorts of cold and jellied meats. His choice of evils finally fell upon chicken, and to the purple-faced waiter with blue-white eyes, who asked what part of the fowl he would prefer, Jimmie said:

"The second joint."

The waiter frowned and went away. Presently he came back and asked Jimmie over again, and again Jimmie said, "The second joint."

He went away and came back with a fine cut of beef.

"What's this?" said Jimmie. "I ordered chicken."

"Yes, sir!" said the waiter, mopping his brow, "What part would you like, sir?"

"The second joint," said Jimmie, with ominous distinctness. "That is if English chickens *grow* any."

"Yes, sir, yes, sir," said the poor waiter.

He hurried away, and finally brought up the head waiter.

"What part of the fowl would you like, sir? This man did not understand your order."

Jimmie leaned back in his chair, and looked up at the waiters without speaking.

"How many parts are there to a chicken?" said Jimmie. "As your man does not seem to speak English, you name them over, and when you come to the one I want, I'll scream."

Both waiters shifted their weight to the other foot and looked embarrassed.

"I want the knee of the chicken," said Jimmie. "From the knee-cap to the thigh. That part which supports the fowl when it walks. Not the breast nor the neck nor the back nor yet the ankle, but the upper, the superior part of the leg. Do you understand?"

"The upper part of the leg? I beg pardon, sir, but the waiter understood that you wanted a cut from the second joint on that table, sir."

Jimmie simply looked at him.

"The English speak a dialect somewhat resembling the

Lilian Bell

American language, Jimmie," I said, soothingly.

A knock at the door, and Bee appeared.

"Should Wives Work?" she said. "Answer that offhand! There is a reporter down-stairs for the *Sunday Gorgon*, who wants five hundred words from you which he is prepared to take down in shorthand. Should Wives Work?"

"Should wives work?" I cried, ferociously. "Would they if they got a chance? Oh, Bee, for heaven's sake, go down and tell him I'm out. Please, Bee."

"No, just give me a few ideas, and I'll go down and enlarge on them, and make up your five hundred words. Your opinion is so valuable. You don't know a single thing about it!"

I got rid of her by some diplomacy, and returned to the Jimmies.

*Mr. and Mrs. Jimmie at Canterbury.*

"Never mind her, dear," said Mrs. Jimmie. "Think what a beautiful, restful day we shall have to-morrow, wandering about Canterbury cathedral. I can't think of a more beautiful way to spend Sunday. London is simply dreadful on Sunday."

"London is simply dreadful at any time," said Jimmie. "Every restaurant, even the Savoy, closes at midnight. I got shut into the Criterion the other evening in the grill, and had to come out through the hotel, and they unlocked more doors and unclanked more chains than I've heard since I was the prisoner of Chillon. Talk about going wrong in London. You simply couldn't. Goodness is thrust upon you, if you are travelling. If you are a native and belong to the clubs—that's different. But the way they close things in England at the very time of all others that you want them to be open—"

Bee entered.

"Excuse me," she said, in a whisper. Bee thinks if she whispers it is not an interruption. "A committee from the Jewish Hospital would like to know if Aubrey will present a set of his books to the Hospital Library."

"If he does, that will be sixty dollars that he will have paid out this week, for his own books, for the privilege of giving them away. But as this is the last hospital in town that he has *not* contributed to, tell them yes, and then set the dog on them!" I said, savagely.

"You poor thing!" said Bee. "It's a shame the way people torment you."

Billy crowded past his mother, and climbed into my lap.

"Tell me a story, dear Tattah," said this born wheedler, patting my face with his little black paw.

"No, now Billy—" began Bee.

"Let him stay," I cried, casting down my pen. "It is so seldom that he cuddles that I'll sacrifice myself upon the altar of aunthood. Well, once upon a time, Billy, there was a dear little blue hen who stole away—sit still now! You've more legs than a centipede!—who stole away every day and went under the barn where it was so cool and shady, and laid a lovely little smooth, cream-coloured egg. Then when she had laid it, she was so proud that she could never help coming out and cackling at the top of her voice, 'Cut-cut-cut-ka-dah-cut!' And then the lady of the house would run out and say, 'Oh, there's that naughty little blue hen cackling over a new-laid egg which I did want so much to make an omelette, but I don't know where she has laid it. The naughty little blue hen!' So the poor lady would be obliged to use the red hen's eggs for the omelette, because the little blue hen laid *hers* under the barn.

"Well, after the little blue hen had laid six beautiful cream-coloured eggs, she began to sit on them day after day, covering them with her feathers, and tucking her lovely little blue wings down around the edges of her nest to keep the eggs warm, and day after day she sat and dreamed of six darling little yellow, fluffy chickens with brown wings and sparkling black eyes and dear little peepy voices, and she was so happy in thinking of her little children that she was as patient as possible, and never seemed to care that all the other hens and chickens were running about in the warm yellow sunshine and snapping up lively little shiny bugs with their yellow beaks.

"Well, after awhile, this dear little patient blue hen heard the funniest little tapping, tapping, tapping under her wings." Billy's eyes nearly bulged out of his head as he tapped the arm of the chair as I did. "And then she felt the most curious little fluttering under her wings—oh, Billy, *what* do you think this little blue hen felt fluttering under her wings?"

"A *omelette*!" said Billy, excitedly.

I finished the Jimmies as an anticlimax.

*Mr. and Mrs. Jimmie at Canterbury.*

It did not disturb Jimmie the next day to discover that

Canterbury Cathedral is *closed to visitors on Sunday.*

*We* saw it on Monday.

After such a day it was no surprise to me to have Aubrey come home so dead tired that our strenuous evening was given up, and we all went out in Cary's new motor-car instead.

# CHAPTER XII

## A LETTER FROM JIMMIE

Jimmie's "bread-and-butter" letter gave me such joy that I copy it here, which shows how little I care for the conventions of life, inasmuch as I reproduce none of the others. Lady Mary's, Mrs. Jimmie's, Artie Beg's, Cary's, Sir Wemyss's, Captain Featherstone's, were all models of propriety, and, except that they are friends of mine, I would add, of stupidity. Bee's—Bee's showed me a dozen ways in which I might have improved my hospitality, and hers, at least, does not come under the head of the name. But Jimmie's! Here it is:

"Wretched creature and your wholly irreproachable husband:

"Ordinarily I would simply write to say that I had had a bully good time at the iniquitous place where you hang out, and by so doing—were I an ordinary man—would consider that I had paid my just debts and was quits with the world—and with you. But not being ordinary—on the contrary, and without undue pride, denominating myself as a most extraordinary, rare, and orchid-like male creature, I feel that the appended narrative, albeit I do not figure therein as Sir Galahad or King Arthur, is no more than your just due. I relinquish the steel helmet and holy grail adjuncts, and exploit myself to your ribald gaze and half-witted laughter just as I is.

"But first, let me rid myself of my obligations. I did enjoy every moment of my stay, and I recall, with a particular and somewhat pardonable pride, that you, Faith, on one occasion, took off my shoes,—a menial duty which I shall hereafter exact of you wherever we may be. Don't complain. It was yourself established the precedent, somewhat, if you will remember, against my will.

"Aubrey, as usual, was all that was kind.

"My duty now being done, I will proceed to narrate something which wild horses could not draw from me for anybody but you.

"To begin with, you have been told that we are building a house, and you know how interested I am in all its details. For example, a pile of bricks had been left on the third floor, which plainly belonged to the cellar. I had to come up on ladders, the hole for the stairways being left open. As the pulley for hoisting and lowering materials was still there, and an empty barrel stood invitingly near, I decided to assist Nature by lowering those bricks to their final resting-place. I therefore filled the barrel with them, and hooked the barrel on to the pulley.

"Now, Faith, as you have frequently remarked, I am thin, but just how thin I did not realize until I had yanked that barrel of bricks over this yawning aperture. The first thing that attracted my attention was the bumping of my spine against the roof—or ceiling, or whatever was highest in the house.

"I had presence of mind enough to kick at the barrel as I flew past it, so that it wouldn't dent my white waistcoat. The rope

Lilian Bell

slid with violence through my hands, taking my palms with it. As I was pasted tranquilly against the skylight, and wondering how I was to get down, the problem was at once solved for me, but not to my satisfaction, by the bottom of the damned barrel giving out. Picture to yourself the consequences.

"The bricks being thus left on Mother Earth, I, with indescribable rapidity, having still hold of the rope, passed the staves in mid-air, as I hastily descended, lighting in a sitting posture on the pile of bricks. The sensation, Faith and Aubrey, is not pleasant.

"However, I possess a philosophic nature and a sense of humour. I realized that the worst was over, and that I was well out of my scrape. I therefore released the rope, and fell to examining my bruises. Will you believe it? Those wretched barrel-staves had no more consideration than to descend crushingly upon my unprotected skull, and to remove portions of my ears in so doing.

"I got out of there. I don't care for new houses, and carpenters may leave bricks on the piano hereafter for all of me.

"I have not told my wife. She is sensitive, and loves me. As neither of these aspersions describe you and Aubrey, I am impelled to state the incident to you, hoping that it may give your ribald selves a moment's diversion. I called on Lady Mary at the Cambridge, and told this to her, and she laughed until she cried. Then she said:

"'Oh, Mr. Jimmie, promise me that you will tell the whole thing to mamma—just as you have told it to me!'"

"Imagine telling this to the Duchess of Strowther!"

"Again, I repeat, I enjoyed myself on your ranch. I particularly enjoyed seeing Bee do the bucolic."

"Give the enclosed to Billy, and tell the old man to buy something with it to remember me by."

"And with kind remembrances to yourself and Aubrey, I am"

"Your slave,"

"JIMMIE."

# CHAPTER XIII

## THE BREAKING UP OF MARY

Prosperity disagrees with some people. But with Mary I have always thought it was jealousy.

As long as we had no one but her, and she practically ran the house and us, too, she was the same faithful, honest, sympathetic soul, who first won our young love at the Waldorf during our honeymoon, but after we came to Peach Orchard and needed old Amos for the horses, and a gardener, and two extra maids in the house, Mary's thrift took wings, and no Liande de Pougy or Otero could exceed her extravagance in ordering things she did not want, and never could use.

I noticed that the bills were becoming perfectly unbearable, and, never dreaming that our good, faithful Mary could be at fault,—she, who used to declare that she had walked ten blocks to find lettuce at eight cents a head instead of nine, and who never could be persuaded that her time at home was worth far more to me than that extra cent,—I spoke to the grocer and asked him what he meant by such prices.

"It isn't the prices, Mrs. Jardine—it's the quantity you have been ordering. Are you running a hotel?"

"No," I said. "Not that I know of."

"Well," he answered. "Look here; here's three gallons of olive-oil you've ordered in one week."

"Three gallons!" I gasped. "You mean three bottles."

"No, ma'am! Three gallons!"

"Who ordered it?"

"That there old woman of yours,—the one that cusses so."

"You mean Mary?" I asked, incredulously.

"I don't know what her name is, but I know her tongue when I hear it. A white-haired old lady with specs."

"That must be Mary," I mused.

"Well, 'm, she said Mr. Jardine ate salad twice a day, and needed lots of oil."

"So he does," I observed, drily, "but he doesn't bathe in it."

This pleasantry was quite lost on the grocer, for he hastened to agree with me, with a—

"Sure he doesn't," and a convincing wag of the head, as who should say, "Let no man accuse my friend, Mr. Jardine, of bathing in olive-oil, while I am about!"

It was very soothing.

"Well, just send it back, Mrs. Jardine," said he, presently, "it's in gallon cans and sealed."

I went home with wrath in my soul, but intending to modify my bill by at least three gallons of olive-oil. To my horror, however, I found that Mary had opened all three cans, and filled, perhaps, but one cruet from each.

Mary's face fell when I accusingly pointed this fact out to her.

"I forgot that I had any, Missis dear," she said, humbly. "I know you hate to run out of things."

"So I do," I said, severely, "but ten dollars' worth of olive-oil is rather too much to forget at a time, and there is absolutely no excuse for your opening all three of them."

"I know it, Missis dear."

I opened my mouth to say more, but her penitence, her humility, the sight of her old white head, moved me. "Suppose," I said to myself, "that, in addition to her extravagance, she was as impudent, as brazen, and as defiant as most servants? What would I do then?"

I turned away grateful for small mercies.

Soon after this, we began to take our meals out-of-doors. I had made a little lawn near the house, and surrounded it with a wire fencing, over which sweet peas were climbing. In the centre of this patch of grass was spread a rug made of green denim, just the colour of the grass, and on this stood a dinner-table of weathered oak. Here, in fine weather, we took all our meals. Breakfast was served anywhere from six to ten, and by looking from your bedroom windows, you might see a man in white flannels, smoking a cigarette and reading the morning paper over coffee or rolls or a dish of strawberries on thin green leaves.

The women—until they had once tried the open-air breakfast—always preferred their coffee in their rooms. But, if I do say it myself, Peach Orchard at six o'clock in the morning is the most beautiful spot on earth. (The Angel has just thoughtfully observed that for me that is a very moderate statement.)

One day while Lady Mary and Sir Wemyss were with us, I made a lobster salad for them. I always use nasturtium stems in the mayonnaise for a lobster, and mix the blossoms in for garnishing and to serve it with.

This suggested the colour scheme of yellow, so I decorated entirely with nasturtiums, and, beginning with grapefruit, I planned a yellow luncheon throughout.

The Angel had seen me fussing with things in the servants' dining-room, and knew that I had made a salad. I simply mention this to show why I continue to call him the Angel, though the honeymoon has waxed and waned many, many times.

Now I admit that *I* am forgetful. I admit that *I* am absent-minded, and I furthermore beg to state that with the Jimmies and the Beguelins and Bee tearing subjects for conversation into mental rags and tatters for the admiration and astonishment of the Lombards, I think I might be excused for not noticing that Mary forgot the salad. She forgot it as completely as if salad had never dawned upon the culinary horizon. The cook, not having made it, naturally dismissed it from *her* mind, but *Mary* had helped me make it. *Mary* put it in the ice-box with her own hands. *Mary* knew how I had worked over it. Drat her!

When all was over, the Angel strolled over to me and murmured:

"I thought you were making that salad for luncheon, dear."

I sprang from my chair as if shot, and stared at him wildly. He regarded me with alarm.

"So I *was*!" I shrieked, in a whisper. I wrung my hands, and so great was my anguish that tears came into my eyes.

"There! There, dearie!" said Aubrey, kindly. "Don't mind, little girl! It would have been too much with all the rest of your lovely luncheon. It will go *much* better tonight."

"You are an angel," I said, brokenly, "but I'll feel a little easier in my mind after I have killed Mary."

It was hot, but I ran all the way to the house. I found Mary. The light of battle was in my eye, and she quailed before I spoke.

"Where was that lobster salad?" I demanded.

She turned pale, and sank into a chair. I simply stood glaring at her. She peeked through her fingers to see if I were relenting as usual, but as I still looked blood-thirsty, she began to cry. She covered her head with her apron, and rocked herself back and forth.

"I forgot it, Missis dear! Kick me if you want to. I'll not say I don't deserve it, but since I burst me stomach I can't remember anything!"

"Since you *what*?" I gasped, in horror.

Mary took down her apron in triumph, and looked as important as though she had a funeral to go to.

"Didn't you know, Missis? In my mother's last sickness—God rest her soul!—I had to lift her every day, and I burst me stomach. The doctor said so. That's why I forget things!"

I stood staring at her. She was nodding her head, and smoothing her apron over her knees with a look of the greatest complacency.

I thought of many, many things to say. And in several languages. But all of them put together would have been inadequate, so, without one word, I turned and walked slowly and thoughtfully away.

That did not phase Mary in the least. She had looked for voluble and valuable sympathy—such as generally pours from me on the slightest provocation. She was so disappointed that she grew ugly and broke a soap-dish.

"Aubrey," I said to the Angel, "how is your memory connected with your stomach?"

"Very nearly," he answered, pleasantly. "My stomach reminds me of many things,—when it's time to eat, and when it's time to drink."

"So then, if anything happened to that reminder, you might forget even to get dinner if you were a cook, or to serve it if you were a butler?"

"Certainly."

"I see," I answered, thoughtfully.

"If I might beg to inquire the wherefore of this thirst for information—" hazarded the Angel, politely.

"Oh, nothing much. Only Mary says she has burst her stomach, and that's why she forgets everything."

Fortunately, Aubrey was sitting in his Morris chair. If he had flung himself about in that manner on a bench, he would have broken his back.

"Mary," said Aubrey, when he could speak, "ought to go in a book."

"Mary," I said, with equal emphasis, "ought to go into an asylum."

It was not long after that that old Katie, the cook, came upstairs, and beckoned me from the room.

"You said, Mrs. Jardine, that you'd never seen butter made. Now I've got the first churning from the Guernsey cow in the churn, and if you would like to see it—"

She never finished the sentence, for I rushed past her so that she had to follow me into the milk-room. (Bee wanted me to call it "the dairy.")

I sat by while Katie churned and told stories. Then while she was turning it out, and I was raving over the colour of it, I heard a suspicious sniffing behind me, and behold, there was Mary, with her apron to her eyes, murmuring, brokenly, "My poor dear mother! Oh, my poor dear mother!"

Seeing that she had attracted my attention, she walked away, stumbling over the threshold to emphasize her grief.

"What's the matter with Mary, Mrs. Jardine?" asked old Katie, wonderingly.

"Her mother used to churn, she told me, and I suppose it brings it all back to her to see you churn," I said, with as straight a face as I could muster.

"Dear me!" said Katie, in high disgust. "*I* had a mother and *she* used to churn, but it doesn't turn me into salt water every time I hear the dasher going!"

Katie is a shrewd woman, so I said nothing in answer to that. Finally Katie lifted her chin—a way she had—and added:

"I'm thinking it sits bad on her mind to see you in here with me, instead of with her!"

As I still said nothing, she apparently repented herself, for she said, a moment later:

"But Mary was mighty fond of her old father and mother. She keeps mementoes of them ahl over the place. She has now what she calls his Polean pitcher—"

"His what?"

"Shure *I* don't know! But she says it is. It's got a man on the outside, and you pours out of his three-cornered hat."

"Oh, yes," I said. "I remember now. What did you say she called it?"

"There it is now, on the shelf above your head. But how it got there, *I* don't know. And Mary would be throwing fits if she saw it."

"Why?"

"Because she says her father used to send her every night, when she was a little girl, to get his Polean pitcher filled with beer. She says she minds him every time she looks at it— Gahd rest his soul."

I turned and looked at the little squat figure of Napoleon. It was the pitcher the little man had given Mary for getting our trade for him, when we were first married.

"She cried once when I put some cream in it to make pot-cheese," said Katie. "And she emptied it and washed it and kissed it; then she stood it on th' shelf with her picture of the Pope that you gave her."

Just then Mary, as if suspecting something, appeared at the door. She looked suspiciously from one to the other.

"I was just afther telling the Missis, Mary, how careful you are of the Polean pitcher you used to rush the growler with for your poor dear father," said Katie, with a shy grin that was gone before we fairly saw it.

Mary turned away without a word. She never spoke to me on the subject, nor I to her.

The next day a gipsy fortune-teller came to Peach Orchard, and told the fortunes of all the servants. She predicted a rich husband for Katie, and a fit of sickness for Mary. I think she could not have pleased each better.

That night we were sitting in the Angel's porch-study, when the most dreadful howls and groans began to emanate from the kitchen. We all hurried to the scene, and there, prone upon the floor, lay Mary, weeping and twitching herself and moaning that she was going to die.

"It's the fortune-teller," said Katie in my ear. But Aubrey heard.

"Get up, Mary!" he said, sternly. (I did not know the Angel *could* be so stern.)

To the surprise of all of us, Mary obediently scrambled to her feet.

"Now go to your room, and go properly to bed. Katie will help you. Then I shall telephone for the doctor."

Mary began to look frightened.

"Don't send for the doctor, Boss dear," she pleaded. "I'll be better soon. These attacks don't mean anything."

"The gipsy predicted that you were going to have a fit of sickness, and I believe it has come," said Aubrey, seriously. "Take her to bed quickly, Katie. I don't want her to die in the kitchen."

The two old women stumbled up the back stairway together.

"Oh, Aubrey, what is it?" I whispered.

"It is the breaking up of Mary," said the Angel when we were alone. "It has been going on for some time. Either jealousy, or old age, or imagination, or incipient insanity has seized our poor old servant-friend, and well-nigh wrecked her. I have tried various remedies, but all have failed. I didn't want to bother you with it before, but the fact is, Faith dear, Mary must go. She has outlived her usefulness with us."

"I've been afraid of it for some time," I answered. "But it seems too bad. She has been with us through some strenuous times, Aubrey."

"I know, dear, and I have no idea of turning the old creature adrift. The last time I was in town I spoke to Doctor North and arranged to send Mary to his sanatorium for a month."

"You are good, Aubrey."

Aubrey smoked in silence for a few moments.

"Yes, Mary has been with us through deep waters and hard fights, and never has she flinched. Perhaps it is her nature. Perhaps she just can't stand the lameness of prosperity."

In a day or two we sent Mary to Doctor North's sanatorium, a badly scared and deeply repentant old woman, and Aubrey wired Doctor North:

"Is this a genuine case, or is she faking?"

The answer came back:

"Faking."

Poor Mary! She escaped from the sanatorium on the third day. But we never saw her again, and though we often write to her and send her things, she never answers.

I think it was the "Polean pitcher."

# CHAPTER XIV

## AND THEY LIVED HAPPY EVER AFTER

End of the story—end of the chapter—end of the book!

And what could be more satisfactory than the ending of the old fairy-tales,—"and so they were married, and lived happy ever after"? Not for them the strenuous adjustment of temper and temperament, of extravagance and poverty, with the divorce court at the end of the second year. In the blessed tales of one's childhood, they married and lived happily.

Ay, and for ever after!

It is a long time,—but I look forward to it without fear, yea, even with gladness. Not that I would so dare, did it depend upon *my* temper, *my* moods, *my* days of ailing and depression, but ah, I depend upon my husband's. He has his days of ailing and depression, but I never know of them until they are past. He has his illnesses, but he conceals them from me. If things go wrong, his face only grows brighter for my eyes to rest upon, nor is he ever too busy or too preoccupied to stop his work and soothe my nervous fears. Disagreeable people are not allowed to annoy me. Disagreeable letters are held over until their sting has grown less. Disagreeable remarks are robbed of their venom by his kindly

Lilian Bell

interpretation. He stands as a bulwark between me and the world.

"And so they were married, and lived happily ever after."

To live happily means for one or the other to ignore self. Aubrey is the epitome of selflessness. So that I claim no credit for the noiseless wheels of our domestic machinery, for over trifles I am inclined to go up in a puff of vapour and blue smoke, and I love my own way.

But somehow, after a year or two of seeing Aubrey give his way up to mine, without a frown or a word of remonstrance, and with such a look of unfathomable love in his wonderful eyes, I rather lost the taste for demanding my own way. Even when I got it some of its flavour had disappeared. Was I contrary? I do not know. I only knew that I began to pretend—I had to pretend, or Aubrey would not have allowed it—to want the things that he wanted, and to want them done in the way he liked. And with such a rich reward! Do all sacrifices made for love carry with them such immediate and rich rewards, I wonder? Can I ever forget the Angel's face when it dawned upon him that I was giving up my way for his? He realized it first as he was standing in front of me, filling his pipe. I saw it come first into his eyes, then tremble upon his sensitive lips, then he threw aside his precious pipe and knelt down beside my chair, and gathered me all up in his arms, and hid his face in my shoulder. What he said I shall never tell to any one, but I shall remember it in my grave, and it will be surging in my ears in the other world. Is sacrifice hard for one you love?

"And so they were married, and lived happily ever after."

That, in the old-fashioned story, was the end of everything. Married love evidently took no hold upon the youthful imagination, or upon that of our little selves. We wanted all the anguish to come to the unwed, and the happiness and dulness of unchanging bliss to descend upon the bridal pair.

Then somebody discovered that marriage was not the end; it was only the beginning, and somebody acted on this wonderful discovery and began to tell the varying fortunes of those stupid, cut and dried, buried and laid away persons, the bride and groom, whom we had hitherto parted with at the church door. It was as if the carriage door slammed upon their happiness, and ended their career. Their ultimate fate was for ever settled. They died to the world with the hurling of the rice, and vanished from the sight of readers with the casting of the old shoe.

Then we learned that life began with marriage. Has our taste changed, or have we only awakened to the truth?

Ask any woman who is happily married, and see if she says she can ever remember anything before she became a wife. I remember that certain things did happen before I met Aubrey, but I recall them as I sometimes try to tell him a dream which is indistinct and somewhat unreal.

But that is because I have found, out of all the world, my mate.

How does any one dare to marry? As I look around me, at the mistakes other women have made, I wonder that I had the courage to marry even the Angel. For supposing he hadn't been the right man! I'd have been dead by this time, so there's that comfort anyway.

But he was!

To those who know the Angel, I need say no more. And even

to those who never have seen him, and never will know him except in this chronicle, the wonder of it can never cease, for so few women, out of all the men in the universe, find their mates, as I have found mine.

Men propose and women marry, but the misfits are palpable all through life to others, and frequently to themselves. They look back and wonder, when it is too late, how they ever imagined that they could live together without wanting to murder each other daily. Yet they console themselves with the thought that theirs is only an ordinary marriage, containing no more jarring notes than most. Yet if they ever stopped to think what might have been—if they dared look into the inner chamber where hope lies dead, they would wonder that their misery was not so stamped upon their faces that people would turn to look at them in the street and stare at the hopelessness of their broken lives. Do the unhappily married ever dare pause to think of the real mate of each, lost somewhere in the wide world, perhaps going about, ever seeking, seeking, perhaps greatly mismated and equally unhappy?

"Two shall be born the whole wide world apart
And each in different tongues and have no thought
Each of the other's being and no heed;
And these, o'er unknown seas to unknown lands
Shall cross, escaping wreck, defying death
And all unconsciously shape every act
And send each wandering step to this one end
That, one day, out of darkness they shall meet
And read life's meaning in each other's eyes.

"And two shall walk some narrow way of life
So nearly side by side, that should one turn
Ever so little space to left or right
They needs must stand acknowledged face to face.

And yet, with wistful eyes that never meet,
With groping hands that never clasp, and lips
Calling in vain to ears that never hear
They seek each other all their weary days
And die unsatisfied—and this is Fate!"

When I realize the beautiful and terrible truth of these two verses, I grow dumb with terror, and turn filled to overflowing with gratitude that, no matter what others may have done or will do; in spite of sad books and mournful plays; in spite of winter winds and illness and sorrow and the bitter disappointment of hope deferred; in spite of bodily ills and heart sickness and the times when even the strongest soul faints by the roadside, no matter what betide, I can always turn my face homeward, and there will be Aubrey.

# Choose from Thousands of 1stWorldLibrary Classics By

A. M. Barnard
Ada Leverson
Adolphus William Ward
Aesop
Agatha Christie
Alexander Aaronsohn
Alexander Kielland
Alexandre Dumas
Alfred Gatty
Alfred Ollivant
Alice Duer Miller
Alice Turner Curtis
Alice Dunbar
Allen Chapman
Alleyne Ireland
Ambrose Bierce
Amelia E. Barr
Amory H. Bradford
Andrew Lang
Andrew McFarland Davis
Andy Adams
Angela Brazil
Anna Alice Chapin
Anna Sewell
Annie Besant
Annie Hamilton Donnell
Annie Payson Call
Annie Roc Carr
Annonaymous
Anton Chekhov
Archibald Lee Fletcher
Arnold Bennett
Arthur C. Benson
Arthur Conan Doyle
Arthur M. Winfield
Arthur Ransome
Arthur Schnitzler
Arthur Train
Atticus
B.H. Baden-Powell
B. M. Bower
B. C. Chatterjee
Baroness Emmuska Orczy
Baroness Orczy
Basil King
Bayard Taylor
Ben Macomber
Bertha Muzzy Bower
Bjornstjerne Bjornson

Booth Tarkington
Boyd Cable
Bram Stoker
C. Collodi
C. E. Orr
C. M. Ingleby
Carolyn Wells
Catherine Parr Traill
Charles A. Eastman
Charles Amory Beach
Charles Dickens
Charles Dudley Warner
Charles Farrar Browne
Charles Ives
Charles Kingsley
Charles Klein
Charles Hanson Towne
Charles Lathrop Pack
Charles Romyn Dake
Charles Whibley
Charles Willing Beale
Charlotte M. Braeme
Charlotte M. Yonge
Charlotte Perkins Stetson
Clair W. Hayes
Clarence Day Jr.
Clarence E. Mulford
Clemence Housman
Confucius
Coningsby Dawson
Cornelis DeWitt Wilcox
Cyril Burleigh
D. H. Lawrence
Daniel Defoe
David Garnett
Dinah Craik
Don Carlos Janes
Donald Keyhoe
Dorothy Kilner
Dougan Clark
Douglas Fairbanks
E. Nesbit
E. P. Roe
E. Phillips Oppenheim
E. S. Brooks
Earl Barnes
Edgar Rice Burroughs
Edith Van Dyne
Edith Wharton

Edward Everett Hale
Edward J. O'Biren
Edward S. Ellis
Edwin L. Arnold
Eleanor Atkins
Eleanor Hallowell Abbott
Eliot Gregory
Elizabeth Gaskell
Elizabeth McCracken
Elizabeth Von Arnim
Ellem Key
Emerson Hough
Emilie F. Carlen
Emily Bronte
Emily Dickinson
Enid Bagnold
Enilor Macartney Lane
Erasmus W. Jones
Ernie Howard Pie
Ethel May Dell
Ethel Turner
Ethel Watts Mumford
Eugene Sue
Eugenie Foa
Eugene Wood
Eustace Hale Ball
Evelyn Everett-green
Everard Cotes
F. H. Cheley
F. J. Cross
F. Marion Crawford
Fannie E. Newberry
Federick Austin Ogg
Ferdinand Ossendowski
Fergus Hume
Florence A. Kilpatrick
Fremont B. Deering
Francis Bacon
Francis Darwin
Frances Hodgson Burnett
Frances Parkinson Keyes
Frank Gee Patchin
Frank Harris
Frank Jewett Mather
Frank L. Packard
Frank V. Webster
Frederic Stewart Isham
Frederick Trevor Hill
Frederick Winslow Taylor

Friedrich Kerst
Friedrich Nietzsche
Fyodor Dostoyevsky
G.A. Henty
G.K. Chesterton
Gabrielle E. Jackson
Garrett P. Serviss
Gaston Leroux
George A. Warren
George Ade
Geroge Bernard Shaw
George Cary Eggleston
George Durston
George Ebers
George Eliot
George Gissing
George MacDonald
George Meredith
George Orwell
George Sylvester Viereck
George Tucker
George W. Cable
George Wharton James
Gertrude Atherton
Gordon Casserly
Grace E. King
Grace Gallatin
Grace Greenwood
Grant Allen
Guillermo A. Sherwell
Gulielma Zollinger
Gustav Flaubert
H. A. Cody
H. B. Irving
H.C. Bailey
H. G. Wells
H. H. Munro
H. Irving Hancock
H. R. Naylor
H. Rider Haggard
H. W. C. Davis
Haldeman Julius
Hall Caine
Hamilton Wright Mabie
Hans Christian Andersen
Harold Avery
Harold McGrath
Harriet Beecher Stowe
Harry Castlemon
Harry Coghill
Harry Houidini

Hayden Carruth
Helent Hunt Jackson
Helen Nicolay
Hendrik Conscience
Hendy David Thoreau
Henri Barbusse
Henrik Ibsen
Henry Adams
Henry Ford
Henry Frost
Henry James
Henry Jones Ford
Henry Seton Merriman
Henry W Longfellow
Herbert A. Giles
Herbert Carter
Herbert N. Casson
Herman Hesse
Hildegard G. Frey
Homer
Honore De Balzac
Horace B. Day
Horace Walpole
Horatio Alger Jr.
Howard Pyle
Howard R. Garis
Hugh Lofting
Hugh Walpole
Humphry Ward
Ian Maclaren
Inez Haynes Gillmore
Irving Bacheller
Isabel Cecilia Williams
Isabel Hornibrook
Israel Abrahams
Ivan Turgenev
J.G.Austin
J. Henri Fabre
J. M. Barrie
J. M. Walsh
J. Macdonald Oxley
J. R. Miller
J. S. Fletcher
J. S. Knowles
J. Storer Clouston
J. W. Duffield
Jack London
Jacob Abbott
James Allen
James Andrews
James Baldwin

James Branch Cabell
James DeMille
James Joyce
James Lane Allen
James Lane Allen
James Oliver Curwood
James Oppenheim
James Otis
James R. Driscoll
Jane Abbott
Jane Austen
Jane L. Stewart
Janet Aldridge
Jens Peter Jacobsen
Jerome K. Jerome
Jessie Graham Flower
John Buchan
John Burroughs
John Cournos
John F. Kennedy
John Gay
John Glasworthy
John Habberton
John Joy Bell
John Kendrick Bangs
John Milton
John Philip Sousa
John Taintor Foote
Jonas Lauritz Idemil Lie
Jonathan Swift
Joseph A. Altsheler
Joseph Carey
Joseph Conrad
Joseph E. Badger Jr
Joseph Hergesheimer
Joseph Jacobs
Jules Vernes
Julian Hawthrone
Julie A Lippmann
Justin Huntly McCarthy
Kakuzo Okakura
Karle Wilson Baker
Kate Chopin
Kenneth Grahame
Kenneth McGaffey
Kate Langley Bosher
Kate Langley Bosher
Katherine Cecil Thurston
Katherine Stokes
L. A. Abbot
L. T. Meade

L. Frank Baum
Latta Griswold
Laura Dent Crane
Laura Lee Hope
Laurence Housman
Lawrence Beasley
Leo Tolstoy
Leonid Andreyev
Lewis Carroll
Lewis Sperry Chafer
Lilian Bell
Lloyd Osbourne
Louis Hughes
Louis Joseph Vance
Louis Tracy
Louisa May Alcott
Lucy Fitch Perkins
Lucy Maud Montgomery
Luther Benson
Lydia Miller Middleton
Lyndon Orr
M. Corvus
M. H. Adams
Margaret E. Sangster
Margret Howth
Margaret Vandercook
Margaret W. Hungerford
Margret Penrose
Maria Edgeworth
Maria Thompson Daviess
Mariano Azuela
Marion Polk Angellotti
Mark Overton
Mark Twain
Mary Austin
Mary Catherine Crowley
Mary Cole
Mary Hastings Bradley
Mary Roberts Rinehart
Mary Rowlandson
M. Wollstonecraft Shelley
Maud Lindsay
Max Beerbohm
Myra Kelly
Nathaniel Hawthrone
Nicolo Machiavelli
O. F. Walton
Oscar Wilde

Owen Johnson
P.G. Wodehouse
Paul and Mabel Thorne
Paul G. Tomlinson
Paul Severing
Percy Brebner
Percy Keese Fitzhugh
Peter B. Kyne
Plato
Quincy Allen
R. Derby Holmes
R. L. Stevenson
R. S. Ball
Rabindranath Tagore
Rahul Alvares
Ralph Bonehill
Ralph Henry Barbour
Ralph Victor
Ralph Waldo Emmerson
Rene Descartes
Ray Cummings
Rex Beach
Rex E. Beach
Richard Harding Davis
Richard Jefferies
Richard Le Gallienne
Robert Barr
Robert Frost
Robert Gordon Anderson
Robert L. Drake
Robert Lansing
Robert Lynd
Robert Michael Ballantyne
Robert W. Chambers
Rosa Nouchette Carey
Rudyard Kipling
Saint Augustine
Samuel B. Allison
Samuel Hopkins Adams
Sarah Bernhardt
Sarah C. Hallowell
Selma Lagerlof
Sherwood Anderson
Sigmund Freud
Standish O'Grady
Stanley Weyman
Stella Benson
Stella M. Francis

Stephen Crane
Stewart Edward White
Stijn Streuvels
Swami Abhedananda
Swami Parmananda
T. S. Ackland
T. S. Arthur
The Princess Der Ling
Thomas A. Janvier
Thomas A Kempis
Thomas Anderton
Thomas Bailey Aldrich
Thomas Bulfinch
Thomas De Quincey
Thomas Dixon
Thomas H. Huxley
Thomas Hardy
Thomas More
Thornton W. Burgess
U. S. Grant
Upton Sinclair
Valentine Williams
Various Authors
Vaughan Kester
Victor Appleton
Victor G. Durham
Victoria Cross
Virginia Woolf
Wadsworth Camp
Walter Camp
Walter Scott
Washington Irving
Wilbur Lawton
Wilkie Collins
Willa Cather
Willard F. Baker
William Dean Howells
William le Queux
W. Makepeace Thackeray
William W. Walter
William Shakespeare
Winston Churchill
Yei Theodora Ozaki
Yogi Ramacharaka
Young E. Allison
Zane Grey

www.ingramcontent.com/pod-product-compliance
Lightning Source LLC
Chambersburg PA
CBHW050035180626
46810CB00002B/723